:::THUGLIT:::

LAST WRITES

Edited by Todd Robinson

Thuglit: LAST WRITES
ISBN-13: 978-1534765184
ISBN-10: 1534765182

Published by THUGLIT Publishing.

Table of Contents

One Last Message from Big Daddy Thug   1

A Bad Day in Boat Repo by Nick Kolakowski   3

What's A Jim Hat? by Nick Manzolillo   21

The Missing Piece by Aaron Fox-Lerner   37

Separate Checks by Mike McCrary   51

The Last Living Thing by Andrew Paul   63

Flip the Record by Patrick Cooper   75

Juke by Kyle Summerall   91

Forever Amber by Dale T. Phillips   103

All Things Come Around by William Soldan   121

Prowl by James Queally   137

Tulare by Blair Kroeber   155

Slant Six by S.A. Cosby   173

Author Bios   187

THUGLIT

One Last Message from Big Daddy Thug

Well, this is it.

The last THUGLIT publication.

Eleven years, hundreds of stories.

Not going to be cute, pithy or any of that happy horseshit.

So I'm just going to say "thank you."

Thank you to the writers and editors and readers and everyone who made it worthwhile.

Thank you, Thugketeers.

Enjoy.

Todd Robinson
(Big Daddy Thug)
06/12/2016

THUGLIT

A Bad Day in Boat Repo

by Nick Kolakowski

Most of the time, clients call me on the phone. This one sent a young punk with a blonde faux-hawk and a white linen suit to the coffee shop where I always take my morning espresso and croissant. The punk framed the meeting as a request, but he let his jacket fall open so I could see the silver pistol dangling from his shoulder holster like a steel tumor. He guided me to a gray Rolls-Royce parked around the corner, where a driver in a baggy uniform grunted when I offered him a smile.

Because I had never ridden in a Rolls before, I refrained from drawing my Hellcat .380 from its ankle holster and excusing myself from the situation. "Where we headed?" I asked, fondling the backseat's plush leather.

"Cable Beach," the punk said, reaching up to adjust his collar. His sleeve fell away from his wrist, revealing a tattooed skeleton, its bony hands strumming a banjo. He didn't look like the sort of heavy you usually found around these parts.

"Swanky."

The ride was swanky, too, except I didn't enjoy it at all. After two blocks we halted at an intersection, blocked by a jazz funeral clashing its way toward the cemetery. The driver threw the Rolls into reverse, but not before slamming on the horn. I cringed at how the mourners spun on us, startled, as the coffin on their shoulders tilted at a perilous angle. I've always believed that if you anger

3

the spirits, they will capsize your life. That superstitious part of me blames everything that happened later—the fire, the bodies, the thing with the severed head—on that honking.

The mansion looked like a kid's toy on steroids, a jumble of brightly colored blocks balanced on the edge of a cliff overlooking the beach. The punk ushered me onto the concrete patio, where a ruddy man in a faded Motörhead t-shirt leaned against the glass railing.

"My name's Clive Stevens," he said, offering a ring-studded hand to shake. "You smoke?"

"Depends."

"I bet it's a 'yes' for some of Castro's finest." Reaching into the back pocket of his jeans, Clive drew a leather cigar case and opened it, revealing a trio of stubby Cohibas. "Thanks for coming all the way down here. I assure you it'll be worth your while."

I took a cigar. "Yacht?"

"Excuse me?"

"The boat in question. Is it your yacht? You seem like a yacht kind of guy, with the Rolls and all."

Shaking his head, he drew a silver lighter and sparked it to life. "Cargo vessel," he said. "I'm part-owner. I need it anchored off the coast here in ten days."

I bathed the tip of my cigar in blue fire. "And where is it now?"

He lit his stogie. "Cuba, outside Havana. Someone paid the crew to walk away from the boat. Harbormaster's charging an insane fee to release it."

"Have your lawyer fly in," I said. "Find the right official, get law enforcement involved if you have to. You don't need someone like me for a squeeze-and-release job."

"I can't do that."

LAST WRITES

I glanced through the floor-to-ceiling windows that separated the patio from the interior of the house, noting the framed gold records on the living room wall, the fancy guitar on the stand beside the expensive leather couch. I wanted to ask what he did in the music industry, after he answered my most pressing question: "What's the cargo?"

"Coffee beans," he said, looking at the ocean. "Wood for furniture, some other goods."

I snorted. "Oh, come on. You want my services, what's the real load? You're shipping explosives, meth precursor, that's your business, but I need to know if I'm boarding a floating bomb."

He shrugged. "No explosives, no chemicals. It's not a danger to you. Beyond that, you can't ask."

That made it drugs. And whatever my personal qualms about freeing controlled substances to travel from point A to B, I had six figures' worth of debt I needed to erase. "You won't tell, it'll cost you extra. Hazard pay. I'm guessing you tried other repo guys before me?"

"I won't lie, my first call was Dennis Smith in New Orleans. Wasn't willing to do what it took, if it came to that."

"You mean violence."

"He said you've broken some heads. I need someone who can do that, should it prove necessary. This cargo is valuable."

"I never hurt anybody who didn't have it coming." I heard a foot scrape on the concrete behind me, turned to see the punk holding out a cheap phone. I asked him: "What're you trying to give me?"

"Pre-paid," the punk said. "The number in the contacts will reach us. You should head to Cuba now."

"Hold on, shorty. I haven't said yes to the gig."

The punk did that thing with his jacket again, sweeping it back to show off the gun. In retrospect, throwing him over the railing would have saved me a lot of trouble. Instead I decided to play nice. Jamming the burning tip of my cigar into his knuckles made him drop the phone and yelp. Before he could recover enough to do something stupid, I darted a hand into his jacket, snatched his pistol, and tossed it into the ocean.

Clive burst into wheezy laughter. "Man," he said, clapping like a seal, "I should pay you to be my bodyguard instead."

"Pick it up," I told the punk, nudging the phone with my toe.

The punk stood there, trembling with rage.

"You'll have to excuse my associate here," Clive said, sounding tired. "He's more used to working the door at concerts than dealing with professionals. Which is why he's going to stop this bigger-balls shit and give you that phone."

Bending over, the punk retrieved the phone and handed it to me, his eyes burning. He would have killed me right then, with his bare hands, if I'd afforded him the opportunity. I slipped the device into my pocket and turned to Clive. "I'll think about it," I said, "and give you a call. By the way, what sort of music you produce?"

He flashed a tight smile. "Mostly pop, for my sins. But I'm ninety-percent retired. Don't leave me hanging about the boat, okay?"

Neither of them offered to escort me out. As I descended the front steps, the driver stepped to the curb and opened the rear door of the Rolls, but I declined his silent proposal. A walk along the beach would give me time to think about how I could make some money without ending up in a Cuban jail, or buried in a ditch with a bullet in my skull.

Some boat-repo folks prefer stealth. They offer a case of cheap rum to the marina guards, wait until everybody's sloshed, swim out to the client's boat, and cut the anchor chains. With a little luck, they're ten miles into international waters before anyone sobers up.

I never liked the idea of playing James Bond in a harbor full of sharks. My favorite repo trick is dressing in a customs-official uniform and arguing my way onto the target vessel. If there are still passengers or guards onboard after castoff, I offer them a choice: hop into the lifeboat for a quick float to land, or stay quiet until we reach our destination. In order to keep disagreements to a minimum, everybody in my crew carries a gun.

After my walk, I met up with Limonov—my second-in-command for the past ten years—at my preferred tourist trap. He sat at a picnic bench in the back, fifty empty shot glasses stacked in front of him, two frat-boys snoring loudly on the concrete at his feet. "They challenged me to a drinking contest," he said, seemingly stone-cold sober, as I took a seat across from him. "Looks like I won a hundred bucks."

"How many shots did you down?" I asked, astounded at the city of glasses.

"Of vodka? None. I had Shirley pour me water." He nodded at the nearby waitress. "Those poor bastards on the floor beside you? I think they did, like, twenty-five each."

"And during breakfast, no less. I'm impressed," I said. "I got a potential job for us."

When I finished spinning my tale, Limonov leaned back, hands folded over his substantial gut. "You think the cargo's still there?" he asked.

I shrugged. "Less likely by the minute. You know a boat wasn't stripped down in a week?"

"So it's a setup. Say we head down there, cut this bad boat loose, there's no cargo onboard? Clive tells his business partners we stole the goods, covers his ass."

"And whoever Clive's working with, they won't care who took the cargo," I said, after downing a stray shot left untouched. Although I'm no fan of drinking before noon, the alcohol soothed my humming nerves. "I bet they're not in the business of hearing all sides out, you know? Clive blames us for this, they kill us, but they also kill Clive. And not cleanly, no sir. They'll make him eat his own nuts like oysters."

Limonov guffawed. "Thanks for that wonderful mental image."

I found another stray shot. Down the hatch. Screw it. "Worst part is, Clive is such a tool, he knows that's exactly what'll happen, but he's hoping against hope it'll work out. Like some little kid believing in fairies."

"So we walk away," Limonov said. "It happens. They can't all be winners."

"Hold up now. Are you allergic to cash?"

"Why you always have to get cute like this?"

I chuckled. "Because if the coke or whatever's still there, Clive will pay us a lot of money to get the boat back. Especially if we reopen negotiations en-route. Even if there's just an outside chance, I say it's worth checking into. We'll just go in quietly."

"The last time we messed around with a drug shipment, I got a bullet in my shoulder."

"And how many times did you get laid with that scar? 'Hey baby, want to see where a nine-millimeter hit me?' You ought to pay me for that."

"Whatever." Leaning over, Limonov pulled a scuffed billfold from the back pocket of the nearest frat boy and extracted five crisp twenties. Placed the wallet back. Stood. "This joint is officially tapped out. Let me buy you lunch at the Lobster Shack, you can tell me about whatever half-assed plan you're cooking up."

The flight from the Bahamas to Cuba is a short one. Five hours after phoning Clive and agreeing to free his boat later in the week, Limonov and I stood at the curb of the Malecón, the road that separates the ocean from Havana's crumbling beauty, negotiating with a couple of teenagers for a ride in their cherry-red '59 Chevy.

Another one of our merry crew, Marie, stayed behind in Nassau to watch Clive. An hour after my phone call, the punk in the linen suit left the mansion in the Rolls, headed for the airport. Marie lost him at the security checkpoint, but I had a good idea where he was headed.

There were other reasons to feel anxious. Waiting to board our Cubana flight, I downloaded a trove of Clive-related articles to my phone. The man had made a considerable fortune producing a rock band called the Dead Wakes. There was just one problem: the Dead Wakes released their last album five years ago. Since then, Clive had gone through a divorce, a lengthy stint in rehab, and a couple of arrests for drunk driving. Nothing like a desperate man to make things a little more exciting.

Well, you signed up for this, dude.

Indeed. I was a desperate man, myself.

"How much time you buy us?" Limonov asked. Behind him, one of the teenagers opened the Chevy's hood and leaned in, banging on the engine with his fists until it kicked to life, the tailpipe farting black smoke.

"A lot. I told Clive we wouldn't get here until tomorrow," I said, climbing into the backseat with my duffel. The perky flunkies at José Martí Airport scan your bags when you enter the country, just in case you're trying to import American imperialism, which makes it difficult to carry in my favorite tools, not to mention my guns.

Difficult, but not impossible.

The port was a standard-issue Caribbean shipping hub: a maze of gantries and massive cargo vessels, along with a few rusted fishing trawlers. Limonov and I had dressed in our finest suits, with fake business cards in our pockets that announced we were buyers in the market for a boat. The harbormaster, likely the same prick who told Clive that he needed to pay up or have his boat chopped to pieces, met us at the gate.

"Are you the men who called?" he asked in Spanish.

"We are," said Limonov, in his perfect español. "We have an auction coming up. Some clients looking for cargo vessels."

"Excellent. We have a good one, just came in." He pointed down the pier, at a small container ship with no name on its freshly painted hull.

As the harbormaster led us on a tour of the upper deck, I excused myself to hit the lavatory. Aside from the new paint job, the boat's exterior was ill-kept, and the inside was worse—from the rusty bulkheads to the fraying carpets. I found three men in the galley, and wordlessly peeled off some American twenties into their hands before heading below. As I headed down to the engine room, I pulled a lighter from my pocket to brighten my way through the dim, stinking space.

You can paint a vessel as many times as you want, but even the most experienced boatjackers sometimes forget one crucial detail: the serial number on the engine, which matched the one that Clive had recited to me over the phone. With that settled, I climbed to the cargo level, weaving past shrink-wrapped pallets to reach the drums lining the inside hull. On the way I retrieved a pinch-bar, which I used to pry the lid off a random drum, discovering it filled with green, unroasted coffee beans. I sank an arm into the beans and found a bundle the size of a football, mummified in duct-tape.

Nipping the edge of the bundle with my teeth, I poured some white powder onto my finger, rubbed it on my gums. Tasted like baking soda. A second bundle yielded the same thing.

"Good going, Clive," I said. At least if the Policía Nacional Revolucionaria nailed us during this little caper, I could offer to bake them a cake.

It also meant we needed to leave, right now. I ascended to sunlight, pausing to take off my shoe and bang the heel against a railing until it slid free, revealing a hollow into which I'd tucked a few pieces of steel before our plane left Nassau. Plucking free those bits, I reattached the heel and continued upwards, fumbling with my belt until the oversized buckle popped loose. The buckle folded neatly on a discreet hinge, forming a frame into which I popped the loose metal: hammer, trigger and firing pin.

From my suit pocket I drew my keys, attached to a lucky rabbit's foot. I unscrewed the brass cap from the fur and tipped a .45-caliber bullet into my palm, slipped it into the smooth chamber of my zip gun, and cocked the hammer back. The weapon had barely any accuracy but it looked intimidating, which is what usually counted. As always at moments like this, I crossed myself before heading through the hatch that led to the deck.

Limonov stood aft, nodding vaguely as the harbormaster tried to convince him that a cluster of slowly leaking oil barrels along the starboard side was nothing to worry about. I tapped my lieutenant on the elbow and said: "Baking soda."

Eyebrows raised, he looked at the zip gun in my hand and nodded. "Can't all be winners."

We turned and headed for the gangplank, leaving a confused harbormaster in our wake. Thirty minutes to get back to Havana, and we could sit tight for a day or two in El Floridita, sipping daiquiris before flying back to Nassau. I would call Clive and tell him that his seller had screwed him over, and that freeing the boat was officially his problem.

It was a good plan, ruined when the punk in the linen suit came up the gangplank, followed by four Cubans holding very big machetes.

The punk was startled when he saw me. "Why are you here?"

I pointed the zip gun at his chest. No sense in subtlety. "Clive send you?" I asked.

"Clive's dead," the punk said. "He wasn't cut out for this work."

"You kill him?"

The punk shrugged. An ocean breeze flared his jacket, revealing a 9mm pistol jammed in his waistband. That meant he had better connections down here than I did, if someone was willing to risk jail to lend him a firearm.

"Sorry you came all this way, kid," I said, "but the 'coke' onboard is a lot of baking soda. Let me guess, this was Clive's first deal?"

The punk nodded, his face tense with worry, and I felt a little sorry for him. When you double-cross and kill your boss, you expect some sort of return. He stepped back, blocking the gangplank while his Cubans spread out, circling us just outside of blade-range. Beside me, Limonov picked up a length of heavy chain that someone had left on the deck and began twirling the end slowly, almost contemplatively. The harbormaster, deciding that cowardice beat valor any day of the week, disappeared below.

"We're going to leave now," I said. "Nobody wants to die today."

He won't use the gun, I thought, with his people standing so close to us.

I was wrong.

The punk thought he was the second coming of Doc Holliday. I read it too late in his eyes, just as his hand darted for his weapon. I squeezed the trigger of my zip gun, aiming for his center mass, and his shoulder spat red.

Screaming in rage and pain, the punk still managed to yank out his pistol and fire three wild shots in my direction. Two of those bullets holed the starboard drums that Limonov had examined with the harbormaster, and black oil spurted across the deck. That was bad, but not quite as bad as what happened next, when the punk's third bullet tore out the throat of the Cuban standing to Limonov's left.

The Cuban fell, gagging blood, his machete sparking off the oily metal at his feet.

The explosion turned the three other Cubans into burning scarecrows. Limonov was luckier. The force of the blast lifted him off his feet and into me, the two of us tumbling clear of the flames. I caught a glimpse of the punk airborne against the blue sky, his legs and arms flailing, his linen suit ablaze as he plunged into the ocean beyond the pier.

"You okay?" I yelled at Limonov, shaking my head in a futile effort to make my ears stop ringing.

Limonov looked pretty far from okay—his eyebrows were singed away, the hair on the left side of his head had been reduced to a pile of ash, his beautiful suit a smoking mess. Nonetheless he gave me a hearty thumbs-up before scrambling to his feet, retrieving one of the discarded knives as he checked the Cubans until he found one halfway alive.

"Where was he going after this?" Limonov asked in Spanish, pressing the knife lightly against the man's reddened throat. "Did he have a boat?"

"Airport," the man wheezed.

"No." Limonov pressed the knife down a little harder, scoring the flesh. "You expect me to believe he was that stupid?"

Meanwhile I knelt to the other men, checking their pockets for anything useful, finding nothing except some Cuban pesos and a few worthless IDs along with a plastic key-fob that might have belonged to a boat. We needed to leave right now.

With the knife biting into his skin, the burned Cuban reconsidered his options. "Go-fast boat," he said. "Three kilometers west, the swamp, okay?"

"Crew?" Limonov said.

"Just us and the *norteamericano*."

"Okay," Limonov said, removing the knife. "But if you're lying, we'll find out."

No way could we leave out of José Martí, not with our burned faces and scorched clothing. I waved the key-fob at Limonov and we ran down the gangplank and out of the harbor, finding the two boys standing beside their '59 Chevy, babbling in excitement as they pointed at the greasy black smoke curling toward the sun.

An ambulance and a police car passed us on the main road, neither slowing, and we made it to the swamp in good time. "Burn's not as sexy as a bullet-hole," said Limonov in the backseat, picking at the peeling skin on his hands.

"We're alive," I replied, doing my best to keep my voice from trembling. Sure, I had jammed a few guns in faces over the years, and even beat down a couple folks in the course of repossessing a ship. But never had an operation gone so wrong. I thought again about the jazz funeral, the mourners frozen in shock, and my tingling skin curdled into gooseflesh.

It took three days to work our way back to Nassau, with a stopover in a Miami clinic so a friend could stitch us back together, followed by a visit to my tailor for some new duds. I had almost no money, because the punk had killed Clive before the latter could transfer funds into my account, but Limonov spotted me for the suits. The television in the tailor's waiting room reported four dead Cubans in a mysterious explosion outside Havana, and I knew in my gut that the punk had survived his Evel Knievel routine over the harbor.

While Limonov headed to a bar to chat up some young lasses and down a few drinks, I stopped by a church for communion, followed by a voodoo storefront, where an old woman tapped my shoulders with a severed rooster claw before sprinkling me with blood. I figured that balanced my karma a little better.

Our feet had barely touched the ground in Nassau when my phone rang. "Are you okay?" Marie asked.

"Feeling a little barbequed," I said. "Other than that, fine. You find the bodyguard?"

"Not yet, but he's definitely back here."

"How do you know?"

"Shooting over the hill last night. The Coral Lounge, yeah? Young white guy walks in, his face all messed up, pops a bullet into the back of another man's skull. Description sounded like your boy."

"Who was the other man?"

"Cop who told me didn't know, but said he was Latin. Sorry, that's all I got."

"Do me a huge favor?" I said. "Watch Clive's house tonight, from the beach side. I'll be there later."

After I hung up, Limonov asked: "We going home?"

"Sure, after we make a stop."

We parked the car in front of a beautiful colonnaded house on Baillou Hill Road, a stone's throw from the pink-walled Government House, and while Limonov smoked on the sidewalk, I knocked on the stately door half-hidden in greenery. The maid who answered guided me through spotless hallways to the rear patio, where I found Emmanuel sipping French-press coffee while perusing a copy of the New York Times Sunday edition.

"What can I do for you?" he asked without looking up.

Emmanuel had paid me four times over the years to retrieve boats with questionable cargo. One of those runs had taken place outside of Port-au-Prince, and I had earned a hefty bonus by fending off a couple of harbor pirates with a Kalashnikov until Limonov could pilot us away from the coast.

"Some guy got shot over the hill last night," I said. "I was wondering if he was connected with you?"

Emmanuel lowered the paper so I could stare into his glacier-blue eyes. "Why are you wondering?"

"Because I think he was shot by someone who took a shot at me, too."

Slapping the paper on the table, Emmanuel leaned back, lacing his hands behind his head. "The dead gentleman is an acquaintance of mine, yes. He hailed from Bogotá, where I understand he served as an intermediary for many important people."

"You know if he did a deal with a guy named Clive? Record producer, lives over on Cable Beach?"

He smiled without an ounce of warmth. "Now you're asking questions you shouldn't."

I'll take that as a yes, I thought. "Clive's bodyguard's the guy who tried to kill me," I said. "Clive tried to do a deal, got in over his head. But I think you knew that." Nodding my thanks, I turned and left. Midway to the car, I realized my hands were shaking a little. Never get involved in drugs again, I told myself. No matter how much you need the cash.

Marie patted the cool sand beside her. "Sit down, love," she said, reaching into her designer handbag. "You ought to take a moment, look at the stars. They'll make all your problems feel insignificant."

The beach around us was empty, cold and bright in the moonlight. I remained standing as I craned my head upwards, studying the black mass of Clive's mansion at the top of the cliff. "Any people, movement?"

"That's you, all business as usual." She sighed. "Nothing all night except that irritating noise. Hear it? It keeps fucking repeating."

LAST WRITES

In the pause between waves I thought I caught the faintest hint of music, three jangling guitar notes followed by the thump of what might have been drums. "I hear something," I said.

Marie's hand emerged from the bag with a .38 pistol. "Shall we go in? There's a gate down here, unlocked, and a whole lot of stairs going up."

"Did you unlock it?"

"No, and I've been here since dusk. Seen nobody."

"Stay here, cover my rear. If I yell for you, come up."

"Playing action hero again?"

"If everything went the way I think it did," I said, "someone else played action hero for us." Drawing the pistol from my ankle holster, I walked over to the small iron gate in the base of the cliff, eased it open, and started up the wooden stairway cut into the porous rock. As I ascended, I heard that sound again, definitely music: *twang-twang-twang*…thump. Marie was right—it was irritating, a bad tune that threatened to elbow its way into my head and lodge there like a barnacle.

The stairs ended on the far edge of the patio, around the corner from where I had met Clive the other day. I paused for a moment at the top, listening for movement, but that damn *twang-twang-twang*…thump made it difficult to hear anything furtive. Screw it, I thought, coming fast around the house's blind angle.

My gunsights found a giant at the railing, silhouetted against the deeper night, his shaven head faintly haloed by stars.

"Hello," I said, my voice calm despite the adrenaline flooding my blood, my heart hammering against my ribs.

Plastic rustled as the giant shifted. He wore a one-piece coverall with a zipper up the front. A hazmat suit. "Hello," he said, his voice soft, melodic.

He seemed unconcerned about my gun.

"Is the kid here?" I asked.

"Yes, but he's indisposed," the giant said. It was hard to discern his features in the dark, but I could see the starlight glistening on his bare hands, because they were wet.

I swallowed, wondering if my bullets would stop his planet-like mass, even if I fired the whole clip into his torso. "And who are you?"

"I often do contract work for individuals with a lot to lose, and a lot to spend. You know how that is. We're kindred souls, you and I."

"If you say so."

The enormous head dipped low, the face eaten by darkness. "What you'll see inside might affect you in a deep way. Ordinarily I wouldn't apologize for that, but I've been in a very self-reflective mood lately," he said. "I want you to know that I'm not an animal. No matter how bad it seems, everything I did in there was calculated for a specific effect. To send a message as wide as possible. To speak to people who only understand one language."

Nothing like a friendly chat with a lunatic. "Can I ask you something, no disrespect?"

"Of course."

"Why the fake coke? Why screw Clive over like that?"

"My client already has his own distribution channels, quite profitable. The hoax was a joke, a friendly way of dissuading an amateur from going where he did not belong. Of course, Clive's employee decided to take matters into his own hands. I apologize, but I really must go."

With that, the giant turned and disappeared around the front of the house, leaving a smeared trail of footprints. Footprints with no treads, because he wore plastic covers over his size-15 boots.

My forehead prickling with sweat, I reached down and slipped my pistol back into its ankle holster. I could have walked away; I knew in my heart that the punk had died inside the house. But the first rule of my business is you need to double-check on everything, no matter how dangerous or stomach-churning.

Taking a deep breath, I stepped through the open glass door off the patio, pausing to let my eyes adjust to the gloom. Through the wide doorway on my left came that awful *twang-twang-twang*...thump, much louder now, along with a faint blue glow.

I walked that way.

Like all music producers, Clive had an impressive listening rig: a McIntosh turntable on its own mahogany sideboard, with the record platter and front panel lit up like a descending UFO. In its spooky light I could see the sleek tone-arm bumping against a thick, lumpy object placed at the center of a slowly spinning record. With each bump, the massive speakers at either end of the sideboard thumped hard, stretching my already-frayed nerves to the breaking point.

The thing atop the record spun another quarter-revolution, revealing blackened eyes, a squashed nose, lips crusted with dark blood.

The punk's head.

"Like I told your boss," I said. "I wasn't the right person for the job."

As if in response, the record-needle tapped cooling flesh again, the speakers hissing loud with spirits.

THUGLIT

What's A Jim Hat?
by Nick Manzolillo

Love is nothing to me but a flower petal, but Snack is going to have a baby, so that means I got to do something. Anything. I got one of my last Reds clenched between my teeth because I'm thinking about how I may not be able to fork over $9.26 for another pack of them. The end is so soaked with saliva, I can't keep it between my lips.

To try and hush up the worries, I'm rubbing my hand over my grease-stained glove box, thinking of the cold and loaded hole puncher I've got stashed in there tucked into a single leather glove. It's an earlier morning than I've known in a while, and with no rest, I got to come home with money—any way there is.

The pickup's got a half-full belly, sloshing around and I think it's funny how that's the only thing that'll keep me from starving, long as it don't go half-empty. The roads are mostly dirt here, and looking at my hands pressed to the wheel, I realize I didn't shower since the last time I went out and did a little outside work.

Sometimes Henry throws me a couple bucks for helping him rearrange the parts in back of his Fix'Em Up shop. He don't got enough to help me today, not even if I begged, or with him on his knees and my steel to his cap. I'm a boy of many trades, at least as many as I've got fingers, but it's not winter or the beginning of summer and Just Like Mom's diner is closed. They don't talk to me anymore down at the grocery store on account of that time I filled a locker with meat and forgot to bring it home over a long, air condition-less Fourth of July weekend. Just like America is these days, no matter who our president be—good men are without jobs.

Snack's a feisty one, and she'll never keep nothing from me, given how she woke me up this morning yelling about how, "The third one said the same thing! The same fucking thing Ray! I'm full of your baby!" Naturally she didn't listen to me about none of the smart options—the flush-it-out pill and a doctor fixing her up. Totally out of the question as she cried and kept telling me how a baby is living the moment you know it to be coming. Well, then I started to not like those ideas of getting rid of it, myself. Ain't seen a child since my sister's husband took her kids up north on account of her being a good-for-nothing drunk and a violent, baseball-bat-wielding one at that. I think I'd be a good dad, but if I want the kid to live with me and share Snack's grandma's pullout couch with us, I've got to get me some green money first.

I can feed my family deer and fish, if there are any fish, for long as need be. There's always ways to get water, but there are other things, other things I've never had—never really seen beside on TV. For starters, kids need toys that are not tools, and they need plastic, soft, furry things. Maybe I could find a cat or a dog for them, but I seen kids kill them things with their wee fists, 'specially when they get to be a hand-number of years old. I just want my him (or her) to have nice, fun things. I don't want them to ask for nothing, that's all. I don't want them to have to ask. And if they do and I fuck up, I want to be able to say yes. People always say no to me too much and I don't want nobody of my own to ever hear that word, less they're doing something foolish, like trying to be playing with my gun.

LAST WRITES

Ashton's not the kind of home I'd say I'm proud of, but it's all I know, and I got some friends here. I got people that always have me the first drink, 'specially at Pollock's pub. And for those kinds of people, I always try and get them their drink first. That's how you know a good friend, when you argue over who gets who the first one. I know others that I see and say hello to from time to time, and occasionally somebody has something for me to do, usually outside of town and over the hills. On those occasions I sometimes have need to bring my hole puncher along when people other than police are maybe going to be a problem.

The bigger part of town where all the buildings are is a bunch of half-circle turns down the road from Snack's grandma's place. I whittle down a second Red before I even reach a road made of tar. Can't much remember the last time I was without so much as half an idea on where I'm headed. Usually there's a goal, a place, something to buy, something to do, somebody to see that has something to do. Snack's the only person, only lady I remember driving around places with without having any destination in mind. We'd drive in a straight line, as in we'd stay on the same road. Not that any of them are straight and not that we'd just drive right off into the woods, even though my truck could take that no problem.

Snack's one of the most fun girls I've ever known, even though I ain't known many more than a hand's worth. She says and maybe thinks things most people don't, and she says things to me nobody ever has. Like she's trying to figure out how I think, like about the stars and the places other than Ashton and how people in France live. Been with her a while now and sure, we fight, break things every now and then—windows, chairs, plates. Aside from Snack's candy problem, which she's had under control lately, seeing as how I had a fist-bruising talk with her seller, the only problem is the time her and my sister got into a fight that ended in spilled teeth and black eyes.

They claim to be friends now, but I keep an eye on them from a distance. Got in between them back in their bad days of fighting, nearly bled myself to sleep after getting stuck in the ribs by a fork I'm not sure which one of them jabbed at me.

Without Snack to wander with, I head to the plaza where the old video store used to be and where the liquor store and market are, like brother and sister. Antique shop is in the plaza too, with strange carriage tires and birdfeeders hanging by its front door but I never been in there. I pull in front of the liquor store and, believe it or not, this place has never been robbed. Aside from neighborhoods on the other side of the bridge, Mobey owns this town. Mobey's the scariest man I've ever known, who never seems to grow older even though I been hearing about him since my days in school.

There might be a mayor of Ashton—I don't know, I don't follow politics—but Mobey is a big guy who owns a lot of stuff his name isn't necessarily on. Like the plaza, like the mill, like the sellers and the runners and the growers and the watchers and the takers and the guards. And the cops too, kind of, in that confusing way where they're still cops but not really—not to Mobey or what belongs to Mobey. Somebody tries to go and rob the liquor store I'm sitting in front of right now? Nobody will know them no more. Mobey's a real neat guy like that.

Most towns, with people like the people in Ashton, they're real shitholes, full of stealing and killing and raping. Round here, you just got the typical fiends and like a gun, Ashton spits its bullets to the other places and towns and even the big city, if that's believable. Little ol' Ashton controls the city to the north more than anybody from that city probably does. Far as I know, far as I hear.

LAST WRITES

Mobey's the only rich person I know of, one of the only real guys with money that I *heard* of, that don't own buildings with their names scratched on stone or show up on TV in suits and ties I don't understand how to knot. Given my current situation and my needing money and all, you'd think I'd talk to Mobey, but I don't know him. I never met him personally, only seen him in the distance, sitting or drinking or smoking somewhere, always in the company of people that won't let anybody else get too close. Figure I've done work for Mobey some uncountable amount of times—instead I know Lou.

Lou's the guy that talks to me, and the other employees like me. He's the manager or the assistant manager, I don't know what the difference is with that. Either you manage with somebody or you manage more than somebody, I don't know. I'm an employee and occasionally they give me work. Lou usually tells somebody else that tells me, and then I go and see him at the ice cream shop. Then he tells me in person what Mobey's paying him to pay me to do, or something like that. I never just gone right to Lou before, but you'd think that I could do that. I could try that.

I watch a raw-armed raggedy boy go into the liquor store. He's pointing a finger at the head cashier Donny, then the raggedy raw-armed boy with his untied shoes is pointing at the cigarettes behind the counter. I can see Donny's eyebrows curling up like the ragged, irritated tail of a horse with a fly fucking around it. The boy's arms are so full of holes I'm surprised they haven't oozed a trail from his beat-up rust box beside my truck right to the register. Donny's bald and ugly, with his nose and ears and lip clipped by piercings. He's funny to look at.

Crank and candy make for unpredictability, but Carlton—he's the guy that controls the guys that do things you can't understand or even know until they've done them.

Mobey's a rock, Carlton's the moss. However he does it, Carlton keeps boys like the raggedy boy in the liquor store from breaking the peace and doing whatever violence he can to get his fix. Carlton keeps over the river, on the stretch of land closest to the town of Brinny. And if you think about bridges and rivers as being borders, then the swampy neighborhoods on the other side of the river are like the moldy dead skin hanging off of Ashton that you're afraid to pick off because it'll make you bleed until you're infected. I never done work for Carlton, mostly because he only seems to hire people who love his and Mobey's candy.

Lou got mad at me a while back, after I beat up Snack's pushy seller, because that was Carlton's guy. Lou had me do a job for free that time, which is not so bad when you think about it. You hear about people getting shot and murdered in other towns and cities when they do what they not supposed to.

There's a car in front of the grocery store with Indiana plates, and below those, familiar, foreign marks. There is a bumper sticker with words on it, and if they weren't highlighted green and gold, they'd be just another combination of letters I don't have the patience to put into thought. As it is, I take a good couple of ten minutes to read the sticker that ends up saying *The cave you fear to enter holds the treasure you seek.*

Something about being afraid and getting what you want makes me think of the people who have more than me and can—maybe—give me more if I know how to ask. If I get myself to ask. Without looking over my shoulder, I back up outta my parking spot and head to where they sell ice cream cones.

Truthfully, I could always go without a shirt, and plenty of folk don't wear shoes to toughen their feet up against metal nails and thorns in they backyards. Winter comes with a shiver though, so the ice cream shop being closed December through April is a typical thing, snowfall or not. Makes sense to me, given how it's more than an ice cream shop called Suzie Q's. I always report to work at that place more December through April than I do in the summer. As it is in the winter, an empty building has all sorts of uses nobody's home will do for.

Closed as it is when I show up, there are a couple of cars in the weed-strewn lot. I remember when I was younger, more of a boy, I got lucky enough to get a big bucket of end-of-the-season ice cream from the guy that used to run the place before Lou took over. I set a fresh Red on my dashboard beside my little white lighter for when I get back, and then I'm taking my cap off and holding it between my hands, over my belly real humble-like as I head into the shop to beg for something to make me money.

The sweet fog of pot smoke clogs up my senses soon as I walk through a front door already cracked half-open. They don't grow weed here or nothing, not when Carlton's swamps are a better place. And being that this is one of Mobey's real neat joints, I'm surprised they've got the reefer roasting so openly. Then again, Suzie Q's is closed for the season. Nobody's supposed to be here unless they told to be here.

That pot smoke, it's like my favorite pillow waiting for me back on the pullout I share with Snack. It folds around my head and then pokes at my nose like Snack does when she says my hairs are showing. I'm walking to a bare counter and an empty glass display formerly full of colorful buckets of tastiness. There are still a few squares of duck tape along the display, and I don't even have to read some of them words fully to know the labels "chocolate" and "peanut butter." There's people in the room upstairs, faint music from behind a closed door. Radio intermixed with static, like it always is around here.

There's a bright blue duffel bag on the counter, stuffed full to the point that if there were anything sharp in there it'd be pressed tight and slicing, spilling out. The top zipper's open a little bit. Don't have to catch a flash of that familiar belly-aching green before I know there's money inside. Like checking a dead buck on the forest floor, I squeeze the end of the bag and heft it up a little. I can't figure how many bills make a pound, but there's a bunch of them, a lot of them, pounds and bills. I tilt my head to look at the ceiling above me—there's nobody around, nobody that knows I am here. There's a little strap along the side of the duffel bag that fits nicely over my shoulder.

When I back up outta that parking lot, thankful my truck engine ain't up for whining today, I don't see any faces press up against the row of second-floor windows. I'm free. I hardly had to do nothing but pick up something no heavier than my lady. Nobody knows.

I'm bouncing, dancing in my seat like the radio's actually playing something nice. I stole. Well, I took something that nobody was looking at. Door was open. Money was there, all set to go. Radio upstairs, pot-smoke in the air. Maybe Lou and whoever was tied up upstairs. Maybe they was being robbed and I robbed the robbers.

I stole from Mobey.

I'm going to have a baby.

The liquor store is a little lighthouse and Donny its keeper. I park in that same spot I was just in ten-fifteen minutes earlier and it's like I never left. Raw-armed kid I saw in the store is sitting in his tan-tinged rust box Caddy. He's leaning back in his seat, not bothering to hide it, being and doing what a candy eater does with his tinfoil and bubbling vial of black-charred glass. I'm getting a nice bottle, not top shelf, but a nice bottle, to celebrate change. The moneybag is in a nest of scratched off, loser lottery tickets in the half-seat behind me.

Still jittery in the fresh, nipping air, I'm not past the hood of my truck before Donny catches my eyes with his. His face goes real white real quick and I don't know if it's because I'm nervous about the baby and the money and that I look weird, or fucked up, or something—but he's white and then he's jerkin, dancing around, raising his hands towards me as he leans behind the counter for a moment.

"Donny!" I call out, barely to the front door with its welcome bells ready to jingle. I look over my shoulder, feeling a sudden quick-thinking chill that some kind of trouble is behind me. There's nothing to my back but the stretch of road and homes and a post office and the bridge in the far distance.

"Listen Ray, I don't want any trouble now, I'm sorry, it, I..." Donny's calling through the windows. I don't make it into the liquor store, as Donny—bald and pale as a fish—is rubbing at his nose ring as he clops a big bull revolver right on the counter. He stares at me a moment as his eyes widen...and then he's lifting that wild animal of a revolver right up my way and I'm scooting back across my truck's hood. I'm ripping open my door, slipping, falling into my seat as I duck low, lean across my driving stick and tap open my glove-box. I cast away my glove and squeeze my hole puncher tight.

"Fuckin' Christ, Ray, you gotta calm down! I'm sorry! It came over me, it just came over me, nobody was gonna find out! She lied to me!" I pop my head up to get a good look at the babbling Donny through my windshield, and that's when I mess up and show him—accidentally—the gun in my hand.

He fires first. Two separate portal panels of glass shatter, the liquor store windows and my truck's, and then there is only noise.

Erupting splinters of metal all around me as my soft moth-eaten seats are shaking, tearing apart from the spray of my crinkling windshield. I'm popping my head up, trying to aim through all the shards between me and Donny. I'm blind shooting, returning the bullets he's sending my way. Not much time to be thinking, but I'm wondering what's better protection, my truck or his counter. Something explodes out through my radio in the center console, splattering bits of biting plastic across my chin. Damn thing didn't work anyway.

I'm ducking, pushing my way back out my still-open door as two puttering pings echo. Donny's firing into the door, and then I'm leaning, free from the broken mess of my truck.

Donny, he's shot all he can shoot—and me, I got three I've not fired yet, and before he can get down good and secure behind that counter, I let loose each of them. I mostly miss as bottles of liquor explode and waste their magic on the floor. I get Donny though, somewhere in his center—he's blown partially into the register, from what I can see, and there's an immediate splotch of red across his middle and then he's falling out of sight. I'll get a drink elsewhere.

Back in my truck, getting my ass bit by sitting on the glass and shards of broken things, I pull away and I know the world's gone crazy. There's a video camera in that store, and I hope…but don't think or right know…if I've hit it. Donny shot first, this is true, at least. Somebody tell Donny I took the money? There wouldn't be no cameras in a ice cream shop, but it's not just an ice cream shop.

Oh boy, people been calling me an idiot my whole life. Makes me think otherwise, that I'm the smartest man alive, at least when I get angry enough.

But, boy…today, I am one fucking numbskull.

I'm not driving by the ice cream shop. I'm not that fucked. But I do pass an older, mid-eighties car that is suddenly pulling a U-turn and getting behind me, and it is green. It's Lou's, I believe, on account of I know he drives a green car. It was at Suzie Q's and is now following me. The front end of my truck looks like cheese, and my face looks like I French-kissed a pricker bush, but something tells me their only concern is about the money. I am a thief suddenly, which only makes me different now, in that the only person that told me to steal or shoot back at Donny, was myself. I suppose the difference don't matter to nobody but myself and Mobey. I suppose, even though I done much in his employment, that don't mean nothing now. There's a saying about biting somebody's fingers and, what can I say? Guess I got extra hungry, feeding for three and all.

They flashing their lights, honking the horns, waving at me to pull over. If I'm a fucking idiot half of today, I won't be for the whole thing, I swear. They kiss the end of my tailgate, and I'm remembering another bumper sticker I read once that said; *If you gonna ride my ass at least pull my hair.*

Maybe I only like that because it reminds me of fooling round all hot-like with Snack, but remembering that now, I slam on my brakes and drive the sharp end of my tailgate right into the mouth of that old-fashioned hunk of steel. They lay on the horn behind me, and I see them two boys, one of who is Lou, fumbling, pulling out guns. Then I lay on the horn too, and laugh, cackling like a mad-dog witch as I hit accelerate and wrench myself free of them. I get something of a distance between them before they start shooting, and I'm thankful for that, as my truck becomes a hornet's hive of metal buzzing on metal.

I think about my kid, my baby, and whether they will have a favorite pillow lying in they lady's grandma's pullout couch like I do. Maybe I'll give them mine.

Going uphill as we are when I hit my brakes, I was going slow—but downhill, I almost out-scape them as I hit a loop that will bring me back through town and away from Snack. I been shot at before, sure. Been shot before, yeah. Shot and shot at boys before, yes. Felt safer though, them times before. Safer cause I was told a beginning, a maybe middle, and then the end when I got paid and told my thanks. Maybe even with a pat on the back or a shake of the hand. Maybe even I get to bum a cigarette.

On my own is chaos.

I complete my loop back through town, back past the package store where, I swear, that same raw-armed candy cruncher is still sitting in his car. Farting wildly, I head towards and over the bridge, where there is no law but the order of Carlton and his candy.

They stop that shooting when we cross the bridge. They smart. Mobey's boys are 'pistols tucked into jeans' kind of boys. Carlton's boys got themselves rocket launchers, I hear. Stashed under sofas and in every closet next to their hunting vests is some military kind of firepower. We are into the thin lands now, full of the dark that is sharp with a rattlesnake's bite.

I take a turn, thinking I can get them with another downhill burst of speed, but then I hit a dead-end street and I realize that I am fucked. I got off-road capabilities though, and they don't. When I reach a row of slum homes and places with fences bigger and wider than houses, I keep going. My truck eats up a small pool fence and a clump of bushes, and then I'm driving, right along beside the river, my mirror clomped off by a tree, my door bending, crunching in as I drive and whittle along the edge of the water. Then there's a big rock I don't stop for, and the pickup jerks upwards, awkwardly, like somebody's picked it up with their fingers and my foot's still on the accelerator. Then there's just the empty, weakening roar of my engine, revving for nothing and nobody. More shots behind me, Lou and whoever is following me on foot.

The truck is jerked up so high on the rock that I have to jump free from my seat. That's before I realize I have to climb back into my truck and get the other clip that's pushed into the back of the glove-box. I'm worried it won't be in there—I'm no second clip kind of employee. I haul myself back up into the truck like I'm climbing a tree. Then I'm crawling, pulling myself to that box of gloves. I find the clip just as Lou himself reaches the side of the truck well before I can slap that new clip of ammo in.

"Motherfucker, Ray." He's breathing heavily as he slams a hand against my door and leans, leveling the gun my way. Like a raccoon in its hole, I'm perched all the way up to my awkwardly tilted passenger door. "I am sorry you found out like this. I'm man enough to admit to ya that I well knew the risk, you being you and all and, and Olly did too. So did Donny. I know and I know, that you being the man—the useful, tough man that you are, that messing with you like that, like this…wish she never told you." He waves the pistol.

I've let mine drop and slide over the driver's seat to the grassy ground. "We know what you can do, and I gotta say, the thrill of it made fuckin' her good. I fucked up, I know, but here we are. Here you are and, you can help me, by coincidence like this. The shop was robbed today after a…transaction. Money's long gone by now, prob outta the state with whatever fuckwad's silly enough to take it, but we got you, Ray. You gonna die, you know that but I respect ya, not that I ever shown ya. But I respected ya, and you gonna be of real noble use after we toss this rig into the—"

I don't do it on purpose, but the sole of my boot hits the gearstick and my truck shifts out of park, where I sort of reflexively put it after getting out that first time. And so, the truck shifts and slides off the rock and Lou, standing by the open door is clobbered onto his back.

With me being as wedged up as I was, I come spilling around both the driving and passenger seat and my gun and the clip are lost elsewhere as my truck rolls back a ways before stopping, back tire hanging over the edge of the running river. Lou's yelling, there's a gun pop from behind me that zips through the truck, once more sending what's left of my windshield over me. No gun, but I got a truck, as I push myself into the driver's seat and I lean to close the door. But Oddy, a short, quiet man I've done a job with just once before, shoots at my exposed arm and I pull it back over my steering wheel. I don't have to aim much as I drive forwards and then back up right into him as the back edge of the truck crunches and sends him partly spinning. I keep backing up the bumpy, random route I came down. Lou's shooting at me now, but the shots are missing, guy is too upset. I keep backing up until I come to where their car got as far as it could along the clear stretch of woods along the side of the river, which is too narrow, and now I'm trapped.

Lou's ahead, and he can probably afford to shoot my way three to four more times before he's out of lead. Beyond Lou's car, there are several white pickups circled around the spot where I drove through somebody's bushes and fence. There are several raggedy boys with rifles, those foreign Russian AK ones. I was right about that, as I've heard. They are whooping like Indians, coming our way, hopped up on candy and the likes. So, I drive forwards once more, right towards a screaming Lou, and I veer just before hitting him. Because maybe it takes more than what I got to hit a man head-on with your truck, even if he's shooting at you.

I turn and then I'm sinking into the river. The truck is stuck on some shallow bank, but it's filling with water and I'm swimming—thankfully unbuckled in my front seat as I reach back, wade the water and grab the big ol' bag of money. There are shots around me, but not quite at me, as Carlton's mad candy-hopping boys clean up the troublemakers on their land. I am pushing through my side door and allowing the river to suck me from that passenger side, with the money weighing me down as I drift off and manage to float free, waterlogged.

The river cleanses me. As temperamental as it is, it's not wild enough to fill my lungs with poison. I let it pull me for a while, and then my foot strikes a root. I get my bearings and pull myself to the riverbank, the opposite riverbank from before. I can't pretend to figure out what happened, but it was and wasn't about the money—which is weird, when it should have been all about the money I took. Lou didn't seem angry, just sad, sad that he was going to kill me. Maybe he was my friend. I feel bad.

It's some plenty miles of walking, but I don't mind. The sun dries me off and then turns the river water on me into sweat by the time I get to Snack's place. Her grandmother greets me on the porch, thin and skeletal as she is. She's got a thick double barrel shotgun, more wood than metal, and she's aiming it my way as I come to that front porch, swinging my bag of money like the bounty it is.

"You ain't welcome here no more, Ray. Child ain't yours and you go making it a bastard, what you did down at the liquor store. It was you, wasn't it? I know it's no coincidence."

I think she might shoot me, but she doesn't. I don't get it. "What you meaning?" I shout back, raising my hands in the air.

"Snack ain't with yo child!"

I get that part. The Donny part? The Lou part? Snack, Donny, Lou, who else? Babies come from love…I love Snack, so she with a baby. No way she love Donny, or Lou.

Lou mentioned sex…

Lou saying sorry…

"What you mean?" I ask again, but I turn away this time, because Snack's not home anyway. The bag of money is still heavy, but I can carry it, as far as I can make it. "What you mean…" I mutter to myself, starting to get what she meant. I head back some of the way I come.

I wish I had my pillow.

Some people turn bad on ya, real quick. Real, real quick. I'm used to it. If I had time and no boys maybe coming for me, I'd get my fists bruised up. But now that I think about it, I already got myself even with the people that made me odd and I didn't even know I was doing it. I wouldn't mind seeing Snack, but the way she says her words might mix me up, and there's people probably coming for me. This I ought to know, considering they cameras everywhere. I should walk, and walk, and wander, alone. I should try it alone, and see where I end up. Fuck that baby and fuck that lady. I'll buy a new pillow and a bottle that Mobey won't be taxing.

I think I'll just walk on my own for a little while, and figure this all out.

The Missing Piece
by Aaron Fox-Lerner

I don't blame my little brother for shooting Richie Vaillard. I mean, fucking Canada, you know? If this were America, somebody else would have shot Richie Vaillard a long time ago. And he deserved it. He stole from everyone he knew, bragged about wriggling out of a rape charge, and snitched out half of Montreal after he got caught with a bag full of heroin. In other words, he was a junkie scumbag par excellence, yet somehow he was still around.

So no, I wasn't pissed at Guy for killing Richie Vaillard, and I believed him when he said it was self-defense. The reason I was pissed at him was because he sold the fucking gun he used to do it.

Guy told me this like he'd done something clever. He came to me afterwards, shaking and crying. I figured he shouldn't let anyone see him cry, not even me, but he was only eighteen and hey—I might be a tough guy, but I've never killed anyone myself, so I couldn't say what it does to you. I asked him about what happened, and he explained it to me in bits and pieces.

Apparently, he killed Richie over a bicycle. Richie stole bikes sometimes, because like I said: scumbag. One of the bikes Richie happened to steal was my little brother's—a nice white Peugeot fixie he was super proud of. My brother found out Richie was the one who took it, got some of his friends together, shoved Richie around a bit and got the bike back. So far, so normal, but then Richie started threatening to kill Guy.

One night Guy was at a bar and Richie walked up to him with a knife and said he'd be waiting to get Guy when he didn't expect it. So Guy bought a piece. He didn't tell me about any of this when it was actually going down, and wouldn't tell me who sold him the gun. Wanted to be a man, handle things on his own, he said.

According to Guy, he was walking home from a party in the Plateau one evening through some of the alleyways in the neighborhood when he noticed Richie following him. Guy stopped, stood straight in the middle of the icy alley, and whipped out the gun. Richie just laughed and kept walking towards him. My brother shot him.

Guy insisted that no one saw them. It was late at night, an empty alley paralleled by wooden fences and fogged apartment windows, no lights there at all, and he'd booked it out real quick after the shooting and then kept walking. I asked him about the gun, figuring I'd have to toss it in the St. Laurent for him.

"Oh," Guy said, "don't worry about that. I sold it already."

"You sold it?" I said. "The gun you just shot someone with? You sold it?"

"Not legally. Just to some dudes from Pie IX." He shrugged.

"Oh yeah? And what happens when some dudes from Pie IX get caught with the gun and the cops trace it back to you?"

He was silent.

"So who the fuck did you sell the gun to?"

"This guy Maurice and his buddy Three-Ball Yusef."

"Three-Ball Yusef," I repeated.

"They call him that because he has, uh, three balls," my brother said.

I didn't say anything

"Testicles," he clarified, in case I thought he was referring to sports equipment.

"What are they?" I asked.

"The balls?"

"No, the guys. White? Black? French? Anglo? They from here?"

"Oh. Maurice is white. Franco. Three-Ball Yusef's Algerian or Moroccan or something like that."

"So what do these guys want with the gun?" I asked.

"I didn't ask."

"No," I said, "couldn't ask something like that, could you?"

"Look, I didn't say anything to them over the phone, just took the metro over to Pie IX, sold it to them at their place. You want me to get it back?"

"No, you need to stay put. I will get the gun back. You use your phone anywhere around where you shot Richie Vaillard, by the way?"

"No, the battery died. Fucking iPhones, you know?"

"Well thank God for small favors. I don't want you doing anything, *any*thing at all, until this is settled, got it?"

My brother was supposed to be the smart one. Or at least the smarter one. God knows I'm not the brains in the family. I'd say I got away with it by being the brawn, but I didn't get away with it. I'd just spent two years in jail for selling cocaine. You play that game for a bit and you know that either you have the money for a really good lawyer or you get locked up. Well, I wish I'd saved up enough for a better lawyer, but it's too late now.

Since I'm the fuck-up, Guy should have been the good one. He got decent grades in school. Not great, but not bad. He finished high school, and he was supposed to finish CÉGEP and maybe even go on to university, but then he started fucking around, talking about how he'd take a year off, finish CÉGEP later. I was hoping he'd at least get some trade training or something. Instead he was drinking and partying a lot and apparently getting into shit with guys like Richie Vaillard.

I knew Mom was already starting to worry about him. Really, I could tell she was afraid he'd turn out like me. If she found out about the murder, it would kill her. I'll never forget her weeping when she found out the "job at a bar" that had let me live nice enough and even kick some money her way, was moving drugs rather than drinks. She raised the two of us all by herself, and she never had a lot of money to do it with. Not her fault I turned out so bad, but if I could do anything to prevent Guy from getting in the same kind of trouble, then I sure as hell would.

So I put on my coat and went out into the bitter winter cold to Pie IX. Maurice and Yusef lived on a block of more-or-less identical three-story buildings in a basement apartment. No one was there when I rang. I went around the alley out back and tried the latch to the backyard. It was shut. Then I hopped the fence and fell in a snowpile on the other side. It made a lot of noise, but I figured no one was around so I tromped through the snow to the door. Before I could try to jimmy it, it got flung open by a little old Haitian lady who looked about a hundred and a half. She stared me up and down before asking (demanding) who I was and what I wanted. I figured it would be best if I just 'fessed up and told her who I was looking for.

"Ils sont vos amis?" she asked me. I told her the truth: I didn't even know them.

"Je t'dis," she spat at me, "ces boys sont vraiments no good. Toujours gelé, toujours font trop de bruit."

I explained that I was looking for something they'd taken, which technically might not be a lie, and she hated them enough to let me into their place to look around. She gave me a whole rundown about how terrible they were, mainly based off the fact that she always had rent trouble with them. They knew they didn't need to pay up since, as she put it, she hadn't technically declared that she was renting the apartment, but fair was still fair wasn't it? And now, she complained, they'd run off somewhere.

The place was mostly barren with signs of squandered cash. They had a PS4, giant flatscreen, and a stack of games sitting on an otherwise empty floor. There was no gun. No phones or computers. No chargers. They were hiding out somewhere else.

I left and started asking around about them—their families, if they had any girls, stuff like that. My brother couldn't tell me much. Both of them were ugly, Guy said. No girlfriends. Apparently more balls doesn't equal more game.

I checked around on Facebook. The two of them were one year older than my brother, didn't post much on their pages. I searched around for any relatives of theirs and messaged them under flimsy pretenses. No response. Three-Ball Yusef had an Instagram. Pictures of weed, small piles of cash, shitty parties with *le squad*, some friend of his catching a tag on a real ugly girl's leg. No posts from the last few days.

I woke up the next morning to see something about a two-man robbery on the news, right after a report on Richie Vaillard's still-unsolved murder. The robbers were wearing masks, so I pulled up the clip online and showed Guy to check.

"Oh yeah, it does look like them," he said. "I think maybe Maurice was wearing that army surplus coat when he bought the gun."

The two of them had robbed a Couche-Tard in Outremont late last night. The security camera footage showed them running into the store at 3:30 in the morning, shoving the gun (Guy's gun) in the cashier's face, grabbing what the news said was all of two hundred-something dollars from the cash register. Then right when they're leaving, Maurice suddenly turned back and pistol-whipped the cashier before running out the door. The anchorwoman said they were still at large and the police were asking the public for any clues.

"So...what are you going to do now?" my brother asked me.

"Go back to their place, see if they're home now."

"You want me to come with you?"

"Fuck no. I told you to just stay here and...I dunno, what have you been doing anyway?"

"Just smoking up a lot, I guess. I mean, like, what's the point, you know? I think Mom's getting suspicious of me."

"Well, lie to her. Just don't go out. She at work?"

"Yeah," he shrugged. "Early shift."

"Alright, well try to be nice to her and stop being so down on yourself. Hopefully I'll be back soon." I pulled on my coat, went out into the cold and then onto the metro back to Pie IX. The door to Maurice's place was open. No one inside. Most of their nice stuff was gone, too. As I was leaving, I ran into their landlady. She'd taken their stuff, she told me. For the rent money they owed. They hadn't been here for four or five days anyway. She thought they weren't coming back.

Then, at a loss on what to do, I started thinking about it. Weird that they'd fly the coop if they were already living in an unlisted place. Also weird that they left before the robbery. Unless they were worried about trouble from someone other than the police.

When I got back home, Guy was still on the couch smoking a bowl.

"What the fuck are you doing?" I asked him angrily. "What if I was Mom?"

"What if you was Mom? Look at you, how could you be Mom?"

"Look dumbass, I'm saying maybe it could have been Mom coming home and not me."

"Nah, she's still at work. Whatever, none of it matters, anyway." He leaned back and shook his head.

"None of it... Jesus. She's at the hospital right now probably wiping some old guy's ass for him so we can live in her apartment."

"It just... I dunno. It just doesn't matter though, does it? Or, like, what you're trying to do for me? I appreciate it, but there's no point, eh?"

"I'm gonna tell you this once because I hate talking about it," I told him slowly. "You do not want to go to jail. I shouldn't even have to tell you that. It would break Mom's heart, and it would break you. I'm not talking any bullshit about shower rape or getting shanked or whatever. Don't make an ass out of yourself, and it won't happen. I'm just talking about the daily fucking misery of it, of being stuck in the same room with some asshole and a broken toilet day after day after day, and everything smells and everyone there is just—stupid, like, they're all so dumb. Trust me. If you think there's no point to life out here, just try it in there."

He'd stopped looking at me by this point, and was simply staring at the wall. I think I preferred it when he was crying. I went into the kitchen, sat down at the table, and started checking Maurice and Yusef's Facebook and Instagram again, looking for anyone I knew, anyone who could tell me where they were.

Looking through pics on Yusef's Instagram from a few weeks ago, I recognized a guy standing with the two of them at Bar Barity. Then he popped up again with Yusef in a party pic from a month before that. The guy was a producer or DJ or something in Montreal's hip-hop scene. He was also a small-time dealer. I knew who he bought his coke from: the same dude half the dealers in the Plateau bought their coke from. Cowboy Jacques.

Cowboy Jacques didn't dress like a cowboy or act like a cowboy. Hell, he didn't even come from the plains—he was born in Laval. He got the name because he was crazy into country music, spent every Tuesday night at this country-and-western bar that seemed like it had been teleported straight from Alberta, complete with its original customers, right onto the west side of Montreal.

That was for pleasure, though. Business you could find him in a rundown Italian cafe in Villeray, which is exactly where he sat the next day, sipping a cappuccino and watching me struggle in from the cold.

"Long time," he said as I stood there in front of him, still in my coat and hat. "This an idle visit or you got business?"

"Business," I told him.

"Keep all that stuff on." He walked over to the coat rack, slipped a nice wool coat on his slender frame, and then pulled a black tuque over his light blond buzz cut and rounded ears. He looked much older since I last saw him, I thought.

We pushed back out the door into the wind.

"You're gonna make me talk to you like this out in this weather?" I asked him.

He waited until we'd walked further down the block to start speaking.

"Listen, if I didn't know you don't have any skin in the game anymore, I would've made you strip first."

"Things are that bad?"

"They're building a case for sure. So, this about your brother?"

I didn't say anything, but the surprise was right there on my face.

"Your brother has beef with Johnny Vaillard, he buys a gun, Johnny Vaillard gets shot." Cowboy Johnny smiled. "Not really a hard guess."

"You sell him the gun?" I asked, voice hard, worrying about who else knew.

"I didn't say that. I don't think it matters, anyway. Is that why you came to me?"

"I'm looking for it."

"You know who has it?"

"Some idiots from Pie IX."

He let out a short laugh that quickly turned into a cough from the chill. "Got that right."

"You know them?"

"I heard about them. And I heard they got your brother's gun. So I told them about some McGill student from Vancouver who's been moving way more bud than I'm okay with from his very unguarded apartment in the student ghetto. And I told them about a place they could stay if they need, just in case that nice hydroponic shit the kid was selling came from someone with muscle, since it certainly didn't come from anyone I know."

"You're not worried that's gonna backfire on you when they get caught?"

"I told them things, that's all. It's deniable."

"You must be really lawyered up." I shook my head. We'd circled the block by this point.

"Calisse, I could staff a fucking law school."

We walked in silence for a few beats, breaths advancing out in light clouds ahead of us. I wanted to get back inside, anywhere.

"I'm guessing you want me to do something," I said. "Then I can get the gun back from the two idiots."

"Yup." He stopped walking. I stopped with him and waited on the sidewalk for more.

"So?"

"I get worried, you know? Even with the lawyers, I get worried."

He paused again. I waited again. I wanted to reach over and throttle him.

"There's a guy," he said, finally. "An ex-Hell's Angel I know. I worry about who he might be talking to. I dunno.

45

He's retired, but he's got a lot in his past to be worried about himself, so I dunno."

"Like fuck I'm killing anyone."

"Ostie de Crisse, man, I'm not asking for that. He doesn't know you. Just…toss him around a bit. You're a big guy, he was never dangerous. Break a bone or two. He'll get the message."

"I've never done anything like that before."

"No, but you could've. Look, I'll give you the address. You just take care of it whenever you decide you need to help your brother out."

"Where's he live?"

"Côte St. Luc."

"Jesus Christ, first Pie IX now this. Doesn't anyone live nearby?"

Cowboy Johnny didn't say anything, just smiled and walked back into the cafe. I went back home. Guy was there on the couch, not smoking a bowl this time, simply lying there.

"Is Mom here?" I asked him.

"You missed her."

I was almost out of the room when he spoke again.

"She wanted me to go to church with her tomorrow. Me. After what I did."

I paused. "She—"

"Yeah, she said it seemed like something was wrong with me, I dunno. I mean, church?" He tried laughing. It sounded terrible.

"Just try and humor her, for once," I told him. "Even when you got nothing else, you still have family. She'll enjoy it if you go, and you might feel better about yourself."

I stalked back to my room and sat inside. Guy had reminded me that even if I didn't want to do this for him, there was still my mom and all the heartbreak she'd have if the cops stormed into her home again, for her second son. Did I mention that the cops had raided her home last time? I mean, I had my own apartment back then and everything, they did it just to fuck with me. Could happen again, even worse this time around.

So I went to Côte St. Luc and broke all the fingers on a man's hand. Just took the bus over there. Walked up to his front door in the evening and he answered and I pushed him inside and knocked him down and held his hand down with my boot and pulled the fingers up one by one until they snapped, all while his wife stood there and shouted at me and cried. Or maybe not his wife, I mean no one's married anymore anyway, but his girlfriend or something. Fuck it, I don't know. He was just some skinny, middle-aged balding guy in a flannel jacket and I broke all the fingers in his right hand like it was nothing to me while someone he loved cried in his own home watching it happen.

He told her even lying there on the ground not to call the police, she couldn't call the police.

And then I got back on the bus and went home. I know I already said I was a big guy and a tough guy and all, but I never did something like that before, you know? I mean, I fought people and I'd done some pretty fucked up stuff while drunk and high, but nothing like that. Nothing near that bad. Definitely nothing that cold, that cruel, that meaningless and methodical in its violence. Never.

I took a shower, standing under the hot water barely moving, torn between trying not to think about it and trying to focus on why I had to do it, and then I went to bed and slept for ten hours. I woke up late Sunday morning and no one was home. I'd begun to feel like this was more my house than my mom's. I went over to the cafe in Villeray and told Cowboy Johnny that I'd done it. He gave me the address where Maurice and Yusef were hiding out, not too far away in Parc Ex. Less running all over town, for once.

I went over there and rang the bell on the door of a nondescript fourth-story apartment. A white kid with shitty stubble and a dopey face opened the door. I could see an Arab kid in an oversized hoodie looking up from his phone inside the apartment.

"You're Maurice," I said.

"Who the fuck are you?"

"Cowboy Johnny sent me to buy your gun back." I pulled out a few hundred dollars I'd gotten from the ATM.

"How do we know that?" he asked, sneering. I could see Yusef move to get something.

I put my hand on Maurice's shoulder and squeezed hard.

"Well," I said, "I know you're here and I know who you are and I know you bought this gun off Guy a few days ago and I want to give you even more money than you paid for it and I'm clearly not a cop, so what else would I be doing here? What do you need it for now anyway, gonna rob another Couche-Tard for chump change? Give me the fucking gun already."

Maurice looked in my eyes. I figured he wouldn't like what he saw. Yusef stood facing us behind him, the gun down at his side.

"Okay," Maurice said as he looked away, "we'll sell you the gun. We don't need it now anyway."

I put the cash in his hand and Yusef gave me the gun—barrel first like an amateur.

"Why'd you go pistol-whip that clerk anyway?"

"He called us dickheads," Yusef said defensively.

"And in English, too," Maurice added. "I mean, this is Quebec."

"Well look at you Maurice Retard," I rolled my eyes. "Hero of Quebec, language-law vigilante."

I went down to the river, found a break in the ice, dumped the gun, and went home. That was it. Nothing to connect my brother to Richie Vaillard's death.

When I got back, my mom was finally there. She was sitting on the floor, legs awkwardly apart, a chair next to her knocked over and pictures of Guy and me as kids spread all around her. Her face was a red, swollen, teary mess.

"Where's Guy?" I asked uncertainly.

She glared up at me. "Your brother is at the police station."

"Listen," I said, "whatever it is, they don't have enough evidence. We'll be able to get him out."

She hissed at me. My own mother, a chubby little middle-aged woman with light curly hair that I'd only just realized was so light because it was now turning gray, literally hissed at me like a feral, angry animal. I'd seen my mother very angry and very disappointed before, but I'd never seen her so contemptuous.

"He confessed. And where were you for all this?" she asked.

"He confessed?"

"Oh yeah. He broke down in church, you know. Something about it just…got to him there. He told me everything. I told him he had to go to the police."

"He told you and you let him tell the police?" I asked her, louder, trying not to shout.

"He killed someone. *He killed him.*"

"That's your son! And he killed an asshole, a horrible, shitty, terrible person who was trying to kill him! He told me everything too, you know. I mean, Richie was carrying around a knife and threatening him. Like, he rushed Guy in a dark alley! He couldn't do anything else but defend himself!"

"No. You know what he could have done? He could have run away. That's it. It's that simple. Just turn around and go the other way. He didn't have to stand there and shoot him, but that's probably all you could think of, huh? My son the big man, trying to take care of everything. You know Guy only got the gun through people *you* knew, tough guy? He always thought you were so great, so cool, so strong. None of this would have happened if not for you."

"Mom, I got rid of it. I got rid of the gun, it's gone for good. I swear, Mom. It's not too late for him. You could…you could tell him to recant his confession."

"You don't understand at all, do you? I want you out. I want you out of my house. I never want to see you again. I never want to see you near Guy. I'm sorry I had you, I don't believe in abortion, but I'm so sorry I had you."

"Look, Mom, I don't even do anything anymore, I just tried to help him for you—"

"I want you out! OUT!" she screamed, face getting even redder, tears streaming down.

"Look, Mom—"

"OUT!" she screamed, banging her hands down on the floor like a child, family photos flying around her. *"Out! Out! Out!"*

I left her behind me crying on the floor of her house, coat still on my back. Everything I'd just done to protect her for nothing. I thought about where I could go and who I could stay with. I could always make some easy money selling at bars again, and maybe Cowboy Johnny would need more things done. Fuck it, why not?

Even as I headed for the nearest bar in exile, the only thing I regretted was that I hadn't taken care of things better. I did everything I could, but it still just ended up with my brother in jail, Mom alone at home, and me out on the streets. Even though I failed, I don't regret trying. I dunno. I figured someday Mom would have to understand what I was trying to do for her and Guy. After all, when you lose everything else, you've still got family.

Separate Checks
by Mike McCrary

She's pissed.

I know she's pissed.

I get it.

But guess what? I'm fucking pissed too, and she can fuck the fuck off if she thinks I'm going to let this thing go without some harsh feelings being expressed.

Fucking please.

One of us is going to end up dead tonight. This much is certain. It's really the only sensible way this thing can end between us. We're grown-up, intelligent people. Volatile? Violent? Loose morals? Without question.

Stupid? Nope.

Jackie and myself have, shall we say…differences. Okay. Fine. Major grievances, to be sure, and those grievances need to be aired. Just like a shotgun needs an outcome, we need resolution. That's why there should be no mistaking what I'm saying to you now. This little bread-breaking session we're about to enter into will end with someone getting their ticket punched.

That's what happens when you agree to have dinner with someone who wants you dead. Not a figure of speech I'm using here. I'm talking real here. She's completely capable, man. Talking, this woman has killed people in front of me. You heard me right, friendo.

Killed. People.

As in motherfucking multiple motherfuckers.

One of us will win tonight, one will lose.

I'm walking into this last supper with my eyes wide open. This ain't no shock. How it will happen and who it'll happen to is up for debate. I've taken precautions. Like I said, eyes wide open. I got here early, grabbed us a table at the back of the place. One of those half-booth, half-table things. I took the booth side. It's against the wall—not to mention it's more comfortable. I also put a 9mm next to me on the red vinyl. Got a blade strapped to my ankle and an old-school snubby tucked behind my back.

This isn't our first date.

Matter of fact, I think we met here. Right here at this same little downtown place at few years ago. Italian joint. This place was our first date. She asked to meet here. Tonight. Oh the fucking mindgames with this woman.

Place still carries the same smells. Amazing the memories the senses hang onto and shove down your throat. Smell of the bread. The sauces. Spices. It throws me face-first down memory lane. As you can probably guess, things between Jackie and I have soured a bit. There were good times. Times sans mayhem.

The waiter asks if I need a few minutes. I say that would be lovely. He leaves, I slurp in a mouthful of red wine and give it a swish.

Where the fuck is she?

I keep touching the 9mm as if it's going to leave me. Running my fingers along the trigger. Like a baby's blanket, it's soothing just knowing it's there. Hope the sweating stops when she gets here. The shaking ain't good either. Can't let her see any of that shit. One: it's not sexy at all. I'd like to hang onto the idea that she thinks I'm attractive, at least. Two, of course, is I don't want her to know that she's got me all terrified. Which is exactly what I am.

Fine.

Scared shitless here.

I said it.

LAST WRITES

I'm terrified of this woman and you would be too, dickhead. If you've seen the shit I've seen this lady do. Scary shit, brother—and I'm the dumbass that stole money from this scary, scary woman. I scorned the woman, and now she's coming here to get a couple pounds of flesh plus the money. Scratch her pesky revenge itch, I suppose. Doesn't matter if I cough up the cash or not, she's already decided that I'm a dead man. Pretty sure Jackie moved my name to the top of her death list a few days ago. Doesn't help my cause any considering that I already drained a goodly chunk of our bank on hookers and good times.

Captured a bit of that good hooker time in a video. Sent Jackie that video. That video of me knee-deep in a good old-fashioned pile of pussy and coke. Not proud of it, but yeah, it's out there. Probably wasn't my smartest of moves since I sent her the video after she got out of lockup. Should probably mention that Jackie was in lockup because of a job we did together. A job we did together to earn the money that I used to fund that sweaty, sloppy pile of snatch and powder.

She's upset with me, okay. Understood. I told you, I get it. But what I did, my little move, the video, all seemed very logical at the time. I wasn't thinking clear then, obviously, and now I've got to answer for my dirty deeds. Like to think I'm being a man about things. I'm here, right? Didn't haul ass across the border, did I? No. I'm sitting here. Waiting. Waiting to go toe-to-toe with little Miss Murder and Mayhem.

Well, fuck me…

She just walked in the door.

Glided is more the word, with her feet barely touching the floor. Jackie is cutting through this place as if the world was set up just for her and the rest of us are mere window dressing. She moves with an unwavering confidence fueled by knowing the entire planet wants in her pants. She's not far off. This place is fairly empty, but she's turning the few heads that are here. Men and women alike.

"Hello, Cunter," she says, reaching our table.

My name is Hunter. She's being playful.

Bitch.

"Hello, Jackie," I say, fighting to find scraps of civility.

She looks at me with eyebrows raised. Waiting.

Unbelievable. She expects me to pull her chair out for her. Not gonna fucking happen. This is a power play and I'm not playing. Time is dragging here. It hurts, but I cannot give in, certainly not this early in the game. She is a pretty girl. That's probably what she's doing. She wants me to have plenty of time to drink in a full-body view of her. This has nothing to do with wanting me to be a gentleman. She wants me to look her over and grow myself a half-chubby. Get the blood away from my brain and fixed on the goods. Get my mind drifting toward the old days. The old days and nights in bed with her.

I see you, lady. I see you, your body and your bullshit. Not falling into your little pussy trap and I'm not pulling out your motherfucking chair. After what seems like an hour, she pulls out her own damn chair. Makes a big fucking deal of it too with an exaggerated eye-roll as she slips down into her seat. She looks great even doing that.

The air between us is thick. You could take scoops of it and feed it to the poor. Her eyes bore into my skull. She's eating away at my brain. I can feel it. I finger my 9mm. There's not a single blink from her. No break in her expressionless gaze. It's as if she's working out my murder while she's staring at me. Visualizing my demise in a little cerebral movie only she can see. There's fire in there. I try to return her fire best I can, my eyes locked on hers. Have to blink, though—that's just dumb. Lock in, boy. The eyes. Those eyes. Those fucking blue, blue eyes of hers.

I try to remember her face during better times. Less threatening times. Struggle to remember what her face looked like during sex. During orgasms. Her eyes used to shoot back into her skull with a silent expression of pleasure. More than certain she was faking all of it, but I'll hold onto the lie for a bit longer, if you don't mind.

"We gonna to do this all night?" she finally asks, fishing something from her purse.

"Don't have to," I say.

"Well. Good." She slides her own 9mm on the table and places her napkin over the top of it creating a little tent. She flashes a smile. I reach for my 9mm. The waiter comes over. She turns to him as casual as can be.

"I'll have a glass of what he's having. Do you still do that appetizer thing? With the calamari?"

"We do," he says. The waiter now looks familiar. Was he here back then? Jesus, that's a sad sack existence.

"Fantastic," Jackie says. "We'll take that and a couple of Caesars to start and we'll split the eggplant parm. Two plates, please."

"Very good," the waiter says.

"Oh and he'll have another glass. Ya know what, fuck it, bring us a bottle."

"Very good," he says, scooting away.

I stare with my mouth wide. Disbelief running ripshit through every inch of me. I'll be damned if that bitch didn't just order the same thing we had on our first date. The fuck is that? This woman just laid a gun down on the table and ordered up a cherished memory all in the same breath. Like it was nothing. Nothing. What the hell, man? What in the fuck kind of mixed message is that shit?

She smiles, giving the napkin a tap. Subtle reminder. There we have it. Smiles, guns and memories. I guess this is the way we're going tonight with this thing of ours. I grind my teeth.

Game on, sweetheart.

"Thanks for ordering for me," I say.

"No problem," she says.

"You just pick that out of thin air?"

"That what?"

"That order."

"Sounded good. Hope you don't mind," she says.

"I don't."

"Good to hear."

"But, and I hate to dwell on this here, but does that particular order hold any resonance with you?"

"Nope."

"Doesn't ring any bells?" I ask.

"No bells."

"Nothing?"

"Just food, man. You sure you're okay with me ordering. I didn't rub on something did I?"

"No. No. All smiles on this side of the table."

"That makes me happy. Hate for you to be disappointed."

"I'm not."

"Wonderful," she says pulling her phone. "You know what disappoints me?" She swipes and touches a few things on her phone. Laying the phone on the table, she turns it so the screen is facing me. It's my video. She touches play, then wraps her fingers together, locking her eyes dead on me. A death stare if ever there was one.

I break her gaze, letting my eyes slide down to the screen. There, in glorious HD, is me working it doggie on a pigtailed Asian girl wearing a pink cowboy hat.

The waiter sets down a wine glass for Jackie while he tends to the cork. He glances down at the phone, getting an eyeful of the blonde hooker with massive fake ones and butterfly tats dumping whiskey into my mouth and spanking my bare bottom with a loud *crack*. The waiter's eyes slip over to me. I shrug. He looks to the ceiling as he pours her a glass of red.

He's a pro.

An uncomfortable minute or so crawls as the sound of the video plays on. The smacking of skin. The groans. The Asian girl barks, "Take it, white boy."

The waiter refills my glass, steals another look at the phone and gives me a 'much respect' nod before he leaves.

The video ends.

Jackie lets the silence wash over the table. She leans back sipping her wine. Her face is difficult to judge. There's hate, sure, but there's something else. Something going on behind those eyes that I can't slap a label on. Something that she's keeping quiet. Something she's keeping special for herself. Yup, whatever's in there is all for Jackie and I'll bet dollars to dougnuts that whatever is going on in that mess of a head is not good for me.

"I have a gun," I say.

"No shit?" she says.

"Just thought I should let you know."

"Assumed you did. Along with a snubby tucked in your back and a blade on your ankle."

I blink. Shit.

"Close?" she asks.

"What do you want, Jackie?"

"My money, Cunter."

"Those hard-working ladies on your phone have it."

"Bullshit. We took almost half a million off that guy. I know the current rate for hookers and blow…"

"The ladies were very thorough."

Jackie slams her palm down on the table. Droplets of red wine pepper the white tablecloth making like an arterial blood spray. She readjusts her napkin covering up her gun. Taking a deep breath in through her gnashed teeth she asks, "Where's the rest of it?"

"It's around," I say with a touch of a sneer.

"You and me were working a con," she says.

"And you fell in love."

"Oh my fucking God. Is that what this is? You think I feel for that guy? Again, I'll say it slowly this time, we-were-working-a-con."

"It was more than that."

"That was the con. Make it look like more. Make the rich old guy feel like a young, misguided girl with daddy issues and a heart of gold had fallen in love with his rich old ass, then drain him dry and move the fuck on. That was the whole thing—dipshit."

"He bought you a car."

"Part of the thing."

"He bought you a condo."

"Again. Con the rich old guy…"

"Not talking about the old guy."

Jackie freezes. Stuck her ass with that jab. Didn't see that shit coming, did ya bitch? She takes a good pull of her glass of red. Resets. Her blue eyes dance a little, then find stillness. She swallows big and asks, "What do you think you know?"

"Think I know about Barry."

Blue eyes go wide, "Barry?"

"Cut the shit, woman. I know all about Barry. Barry, the guy you were fucking while you were working the rich old guy con and working me." I take reassuring gulp of red and ask, "Barry? Barry ringing any bells, sweetheart?"

"Fine. So there's a Barry."

"So there's a Barry? That really just slide off your filthy-ass tongue?"

"Doesn't justify you sending a clip of you crushing ass as I'm walking out of county after a prostitution rap."

Can't help but giggle on that one. Might have actually snorted.

"Funny? This funny to you? You left me high and dry when the old guy died on top of me, inside of me, and then the cops kick in the motel room door. While we're talking all friendly like, how the hell did the cops show up exactly?"

"They are amazing aren't they? Those cops man…"

"Fuck you."

"Nice talk, sugar-mouth."

"Barry is outside."

"What?"

"Barry is outside with five guys. Big guys. Big guys with tools. You are not leaving here alive. So you need to give up the money or we're gonna to start at your little piggies and work our way up."

"Doesn't sound good."

"Promise you won't dig it."

I fake a terror-shiver and say, "Spooky."

"Smug fucking…"

My cell buzzes. I put up a finger requesting a moment to answer. Jackie can't believe I'm taking a call right now, but I answer it anyway.

"Yeah…right…cool." I place my hand over the phone and ask Jackie, "How many guys, minus Barry? You said five, right?"

Jackie's face goes slack. Blues go dead.

"You remember Ronnie and the Jigsaw Brothers?"

She nods with eyebrows raised.

I tap speaker on my phone and say, "Ronnie. You there?"

"I am," says Ronnie.

"Got you on speaker with me and Jackie."

"Oh hey Jackie. Long time."

"Hey Ronnie," she mutters.

I ask, "Ronnie? How many guys you and the Jigsaw Brothers take down outside?"

"Ahh let me count—I got six in all. Yukon is stuffed full of big-ass dead bastards."

"Six? That include that fuckstick, Barry?"

"It does. He was scrappy."

Jackie's face drops.

"Thanks, Ronnie. Be well."

"Peace," Ronnie says hanging up.

I touch END. Smile big as shit. I'm enjoying this moment. Feels damn good. Power tilting my way for once.

I feel something cold. Something cold pressing against my temple. I turn seeing the waiter taking a seat next to me while holding a gun to my head. He's kind enough to refill my wine with his free hand, however.

"How many guys are you fucking these days?" I ask Jackie.

"Hopefully enough," she says.

I look around the restaurant. It's empty. I say, "Thought I recognized your bitch ass. You're the owner?"

"Guilty," he says.

"You clear the place out? Give the kitchen the rest of the night off?" I ask the waiter.

"I did. Dead dudes upset the public and the staff."

"Where's the damn money?" barks Jackie.

I close my eyes and take in a deep, deep breath. "There's about three hundred grand and some change left. And before you ask, I can get to it."

"Good. Now tell Ronnie and the Jigsaws to stand down and we'll go get it," she says.

"No," I say.

"Pardon?" asks Jackie.

The waiter presses the gun harder to my head.

"Counter offer," I say.

The waiter shakes his head in disgust. He looks to Jackie for his orders.

"This should be good," she says.

"You get a hundred. I take the two. The change falls to Ronnie and the Jigsaws. Good people, all of them, not cheap, however…"

"Think you're missing the point of my gun," the waiter says.

"One-fifty each," she says.

"Baby? You're--what? Negotiating with this clown?" Waiter says.

"Baby?" I say.

"Focus," Jackie says.

"Fine," I say, "but the waiter dies."

The waiter snorts.

Jackie blinks then, "Fine."

"What? Wait a fucking…"

LAST WRITES

Blam. Jackie puts a bullet in his handsome, dumb little head. He slump-rolls to the floor in a pulpy mess. Jackie places her 9mm back down on the table. Doesn't bother with the napkin this time.

I take a sip from my wine. She takes a drink as well. We share a look. I smile. She smiles back. The girl can light up a room when she wants to. There's a lot of history here. A lot shared between us. Hard to envision this working out. Her and I. Trust issues and so on, but there was something there. Still is even after all this unfortunate shit. Like the thing between us never left. Well, maybe it left for a little while. Pressed pause let's say.

"You think they got the calamari done before they left?" I ask.

"Maybe. Should we check the kitchen?"

"Yeah, let's change tables though," I say thumbing towards the dead waiter's spitting head wound.

I put my hand out. She wraps her fingers around mine as I escort her back to the kitchen. I know damn well she has something else planned. She'll probably try to kill me later, but right now, at this moment, this is nice.

Like it used to be. Just us. Jackie and Hunter against the world.

Yeah, I like that shit.

Real nice.

She's going to be so fucking pissed when she finds out there's no money.

The Last Living Thing

by Andrew Paul

Duchamp guided the outboard motor as it churned the green-gray water, eyeing the woman seated in front of him while she picked at hull rust in between sips from her canteen. He was almost certain Sara sensed his furtive stare as he searched for the subtlest discomfort, for some tell of hesitation. Even the sunlight broke into wide-eyed refractions as it hit the water, as if suspicious of her presence in what was, until recently, an abandoned spit of swampland.

Sara's arm shot towards the back of her neck a few minutes later, slapping at whatever she felt crawling across her skin. The canteen knocked from her lap into the water, and Duchamp let it bob away on the boat's speed wake. She examined her hand—only sweat. Duchamp's throaty laugh cut above the flatulent engine, its puttering gurgle resembling a schoolroom taunt. Sara turned backwards, face flushed from heat and embarrassment.

"Almost there," Duchamp said, still smiling.

Sara spun back around, peering over the side of the small transport to confirm her guide's estimate. Patches of oily sheen coated the water, their reflections distorted in hues the color of deep bruises. Duchamp eased the motor down, and they slowed around a bend in the course, cypress trunks thinning towards a large, circular clearing in the distance. The trees eventually stopped altogether, forming a lake's perimeter roughly the size of a football field. The boat drifted into it.

The air was near silent except for whispered bubbling, and Duchamp scanned the water. His eyes passed over innumerable gaseous pockets seeping up to the surface. The air smelled toxic—a mix of tar, sulfur, and wet earth. Sara dug a camera out of her bag and began snapping test pictures, swapping between various lenses. The results apparently weren't satisfying, and she scooted forward on her knees, both hands occupied with steadying her framing.

"Careful. You don' want to get too close to them fumes," cautioned Duchamp.

She nodded without breaking concentration, reaching down with one hand to draw the bandanna wrapped around her neck over her nose, outlaw-style. Duchamp leaned back against the outboard and began humming to himself.

"What is all that seeping up?" Sara asked, muffled by the cloth covering her mouth.

"Nothing good. They gave us a list with all the names when they made Ledoux evacuate," said Duchamp.

"When did they say it was safe to come back home?"

Duchamp snorted and stared off towards the lake border, his reply sufficient. Sara lowered the camera, scrolling through the images.

A strained creak followed by a snap in the distance. Duchamp sat up stiffly, pointing in the direction of the noise. "Over there, ten o'clock," he said.

Sara followed his line of sight and began squeezing off pictures. Small rapids formed near the dying cypress at the boundary's far edge. One of the trunks fell backwards as it sank, as if someone pulled a rug out from under it. Another followed, then another as the bayou churned momentarily, then calmed. The bubbles resumed popping as if belching after a meal.

"It been taking down a couple every other day or so. Sucks them right under." Duchamp snapped calloused fingertips. "It slow, but it getting bigger, that's for sure."

"Can we get any farther out?"

Duchamp sucked at the corner of his lip, scratching his jaw through a tangle of copper-colored beard. "I suppose," he concluded, turning back to crank the motor.

After a few sputterings, the engine came to life, and Duchamp piloted them towards the center of the clearing. Sara continued taking in everything through her lens.

"When's the last time you heard from Westerfield?" she asked.

"Bout six weeks ago, around Fourth of July. Back when they said the reimbursements were about to end," said Duchamp.

Sara paused to fish a notebook and pen from her back pocket, and began scribbling. She shook her head. "So they're not paying you anymore?"

"Hell, they barely paid us to begin with. Courts ordered them the minimum reparations. Said..." Duchamp paused, looking upwards while squinting to recall the exact words, "...As of now, the exact cause of the drilling collapse cannot be directly attributed to Westerfield Chemical, but certain community safeguards were undoubtedly ignored." Duchamp spat into the water, his saliva breaking up an oil slick. "Or something to that effect."

A thick breeze carrying a decayed stench rolled across the boat, seeming to amplify the heat. Sara's brow creased, hinting at the nausea roiling up in her stomach. She gripped the boat's edge with both hands, and her knuckles blanched.

"Yeah, why don't we head over to the homes? I don't know how good it is to stick around here long," Duchamp said, kicking the motor back to life before Sara could protest.

She swallowed the vomit in her throat while shrinking back into the boat, settling against a backrest.

"Most everything and everyone I know is rotten since the collapse," said Duchamp. He wiped his nose on his sleeve. "It's in the blood of things now."

It took less than ten minutes to navigate away from the bayou wastes into a tributary stream running along a line of shotgun trailers. Paint-chipped swing sets rocked slightly in the stagnant air while clotheslines, some still draped with sun-bleached shirts and jeans, rose out of overgrown backyard lawns like unearthed bone. Duchamp's kitchen windows still had their sheer curtains drawn, and he felt unwelcome and unfamiliar despite a lifetime of loving this place.

For a moment, he thought he saw the silhouette of someone standing there, peering back out at him, wary of these intruders atop the waters. The gossamer curtain fabric stuck against its dingy, greased features as it leaned towards the glass. He heard the crack of another tree in the distance as the shadow pressed one viscous palm on the window—or was it the sound of splitting glass, the figure pushing hard to break loose of Duchamp's home? Sun glare passed over the reflection, and it was gone.

"Which one was yours?" Sara asked, lowering the bandanna.

Duchamp pointed. He heard the camera click. Without thinking, he turned towards the embankment. "Wanna go inside?" he asked without changing his course.

Sara didn't answer, and it was now Duchamp who felt eyes on him. He broke his concentration away from the steering to look at her.

"We'll be fine," he assured. "Patrol come through here maybe twice a week nowadays, usually at night."

No one wanted to be anywhere near the Ladoux collapse—Duchamp included. He'd only done these excursions twice before since the disaster, and only when Angie's hospital bills started keeping him up at night.

LAST WRITES

Three hundred dollars a trip plus expenses for two hours inside the evacuated zone. Both previous customers touted the same thing; trying to write some career-making tell-all about the ignored, impoverished bayou community swallowed whole by ecological catastrophe. He never saw the first of the articles. The second, barely a blip on some highbrow magazine's blog, was mostly about the writer's issues with his dad. What little space was devoted to Ladoux ended up inaccurate trash, anyway. Among other things, the piece claimed Ladoux residents were developing cancer—which, as far as Duchamp could tell, wasn't true. No one knew what they were developing.

They sidled up to land, and Sara eased out of the boat onto the lawn, Duchamp steadying himself while following after her. The air was empty of summer life. No birds, no gnats. No splash from fish fin. The poisoned system could barely support what little existence remained. Duchamp stopped after a few dusty, noisome steps and looked down. The brittle grass powdering beneath his boots. Sara continued ahead, bending down to photograph different angles of a deflated kiddie pool, its plastic rotting away like dead skin to reveal earthen innards.

Duchamp studied his ward as she stood to scan the bayou behind him. She was very young, very pretty. A journalist, but surely only recently so. When she told him the publication she wrote for, he asked for proof before agreeing to shepherd Sara to the collapse. He felt that he could wander this ruined landscape without notice—the life he once lived here was etched into his worn, tan-taut skin. Duchamp blended in so completely, he wondered if an outsider like Sara would have even picked him out of the bayou emptiness without his guidance. This woman in front of him, Sara, was the last living thing in Ladoux. In the surrounding blight, she was anathema.

"When was the last time you were in your home?" she asked, drawing him back into the moment.

He glanced over her shoulder at the trailer. Recovery surveyors had scribbled some indecipherable phrase above the door in runny paint.

"Day I left," he said, and walked towards the entrance. "Looks the same," he lied.

It was only after Duchamp opened the outer screen that he remembered he didn't have his house keys on him. He hadn't expected to ever use them again, and tried unsuccessfully to jimmy the door handle with his pocketknife. It took a few shoulder slams, but in time he broke open the shoddy bolt lock, half-stumbling into the stale-smelling, oven-hot living room. Almost immediately, beads of sweat formed on the back of his neck and across his large, paunchy stomach. He instinctively reached for the fan switch, flicking it on and off a couple times before remembering the power hadn't been on for over a year. Sara murmured something and started clicking away with her camera.

Duchamp's eyes adjusted to the dimness, taking in everything wrong with the room. Nothing was out of place, but there was an unfamiliarity to it that made him uneasy, like all of his possessions had been replaced with replicas. He stepped farther inside to give Sara the space to move around, and headed to the right, towards the kitchen where he'd seen the shadow staring back through the window.

"Do you smell that?" Sara asked from the next room.

"Whatever was left in the fridge," he explained, noting the sink piled with dishes caked in cemented food scraps.

He lifted one with the opened blade of his pocketknife, and seeing the back half of a dead roach in the drain, eased the plate down with a small clatter. Sunlight glinted off a laminated surface at the corner of Duchamp's eye, and he turned toward it. A photo still stuck to the fridge door—Angie in front of a small Christmas tree bowing under the weight of its ornaments. Their first anniversary, thirty years back. She wore her thin

68

necklace, a present from him she opened early. There was a vitality in her eyes that went beyond youth.

He used to think that's what kept him up often while lying in bed next to her. When he couldn't sleep, Duchamp would watch her do so instead, staring at an invisible glow behind her eyes so bright that he sometimes could barely stand it. Angie possessed that glint until they left this place. Her sleep, induced and uninterrupted, housed none of that fire now. He lifted the magnet pinning the picture, and pocketed it.

There was what sounded like a muffled concussion from the other end of the trailer, but Sara didn't look up from her camera. Another bump.

"Did you hear that?" Duchamp asked.

"Hmm?" Sara said, absorbed in her documentation.

The noise again, louder. Duchamp squinted down the hallway into his and Angie's bedroom. A creak of flooring preceded someone's thin shape crossing the doorway. Duchamp strode through the trailer, lightly pushing Sara aside, knife still in hand.

"What?" Sara said, drawing a sharp, startled breath.

"Stay there," he said, commanding both her and the stranger.

His room was barely bigger than the bed in its center, and it took little time to confirm its emptiness. There was no closet to hide in, so Duchamp knelt, flipping the blankets over the mattress edge, but found nothing underneath. He looked up, startled to find Sara standing in the hall, holding her camera at her side.

"What's the matter?" she asked.

"Nothing, sorry. Thought I heard someone," said Duchamp.

He took a seat on the mattress and began surveying the room.

"Would anyone still be around?" Sara said.

"No." He opened and closed a bedside drawer. "Will people read it?" he asked her, trying to shift conversation.

"I hope so," said Sara, adding, "That's the plan, I mean."

Duchamp nodded, brushing his hands over the sheets.

"It's hard to make people care about a place like this," he said, more to himself than her.

Sara stared at him.

"People only be interested in rich American kid tourists doing bad things overseas. White toddlers kidnapped in the daylight. Violence against sweet people. Those sort of stuff." Duchamp looked at his nightstand, still cluttered with his past life's detritus. Scraps of paper, a dusty water glass, a ten-dollar wristwatch. "That's the only sadness that makes the TV. Whole trailer trash town ate up overnight, nobody cares. All I hear been, 'Dumbass hicks shouldn't have lived in the swamp,' and such."

"I don't think that, if it helps," Sara offered.

"Appreciated," he said with a thin smile.

A silence fell into the room, and Sara looked at her phone before excusing herself, allowing Duchamp some time alone with it. He slid sideways onto the pillows, burying his face in them. Inhaling carried a ghost scent of Angie's hair, and he fought the urge to weep.

The screen hinges creaked open in the living room, ending both the quiet and Duchamp's spiral. He got up just in time to see Sara's arm closing the door behind her as she walked outside. The door shut, and in the shadows behind it stood a thin, wavering silhouette. Duchamp froze while the figure's haze focused into an oily sheen, skin dancing like the surface of a soap bubble before bursting into nothingness, accompanied by a sound like straining branches or fracturing bones. He blinked and found himself laying across the bedding again, wondering if he had dozed off for a moment.

He exited his home to find Sara pacing circles in the yard, alternating between holding a cell phone to her ear and staring at it, frustrated.

"No service gonna be out here," he said.

She held out a finger, then cupped the speaker with her other hand.

"Voicemail," she mouthed to him before turning away. "Hey, sorry I missed your call earlier. Trip is going well, I'm actually out at Ladoux now. It's definitely something." A glance at Duchamp. "I'll try again later tonight. Hope Dad's feeling better. Love you."

Duchamp checked his watch, looked towards the setting sun. If they left now, he might still make it back to Angie before visitation hours ended.

"Probably bout time to head back," he suggested.

"Sure thing," she said, adjusting her camera for a few last pictures.

He walked towards the boat, trying reconcile the shadow figures in his home. Duchamp didn't believe in ghosts, but he understood what it meant to be haunted. The only space between life and death was within one's final exhalation, that last breath declaring an end to a voice, and the beginning of its echo. He felt the reverberations were what stayed with you, not the souls. There was no Heaven to wander for the dead, only a world left behind for the living, listening to these whispers as their lungs filled and emptied and refilled in an atmosphere of last breaths.

Navigating these thoughts, Duchamp briefly lost his footing on the slick, muddy banks and tripped, his right knee and both hands landing in swamp mire. A thin, deformed outline in the cloudy water stared back at him.

"Oh. You okay, Mr. Duchamp?" Sara asked. He heard her jogging to his side and raised a hand to stop her.

"I'm fine." He forced a laugh. "Just clumsy. I forgot how slippery this place is."

Duchamp grabbed the side of the boat, helping himself back up and into the hull. He took a seat near the motor, then waved Sara forward.

"You sure you're not hurt?" she said.

"I'll feel it tomorrow, but it fine now."

She got in, surveying Duchamp then Ladoux's trailer park one more time as Duchamp fired up the engine, backing them out into the waters. He took a last look at his home as he tried wiping his hands on his jeans, but an oily sap stuck to his palms. He stared at them, trying to understand how the world out there and its currents would continue to ripple and flow as the waters here remained stagnant.

As they rode into the Ladoux collapse again, Duchamp studied Sara's profile, beautiful and young and expressive. A face people remember, eyes that glowed in dusk light. The knowledge hit him, and he understood as much as he didn't want to. He grimaced and reached for his knife.

"What's the matter?" Sara asked as he cut the motor off.

"I'm very sorry," Duchamp said, and lunged at her.

The knife went in easy, under the rib cage, and Sara let out a heavy groan. Duchamp retracted the blade, and Sara tried gouging at his eyes. A thumb jabbed into his left socket, and he fell backwards, Sara's weight collapsing on top of him.

"No," she sputtered.

"I'm sorry," repeated Duchamp, trying to find the knife knocked out of his hand in the struggle.

Sara grabbed his neck, choking him while pushing his face sideways towards the boat floor. The stench of silt and chemicals and blood, and Duchamp gagged while trying to kick out from under the woman. She struck him in his stomach, each punch weaker than the last until he barely felt them at all. The last one almost felt tender.

The world began to darken briefly, but Sara's grip slackened. Duchamp closed his eyes, and heaved himself upward, taking her head in one hand and slamming it against the edge of the rusted hull. Any remaining fight left her then, and she crumpled into the violently rocking boat, her body starting to spasm as blood seeped into her hair.

Duchamp caught his breath for a minute, then leaned over her, his hands reaching under Sara's frame to lift her up. Her eyes followed his movements, but her glow was all but extinguished. Duchamp rolled her overboard, offering her to the collapse like a sacrifice to a god he both didn't understand and feared.

Leaning over the boat's edge, he watched a dark, shimmering reflection in the poisoned water, faceless and contorted. Sara, on her back, sank feet first, until her face was the last visible portion—until the bayou washed over her, lowering her under like a baptismal.

He coughed, and felt a shock tear through his right side. Duchamp looked down to find his knife embedded in his stomach. There wasn't much apart from the hot pain as his senses began failing him, and he slumped over against the motor. His wasn't able to grab the Christmas photo from his pocket with his hands shaking as they were, so he simply watched as the blood pumped out of him in small waves. His vision blurred, but not before Duchamp saw the ripples traveling across the water, away from the boat's brief, sudden violence.

He imagined them strong enough to reach the world, to make people realize that there was, at one time, a place full of true life here in the swamps. They might not notice him gone, but sooner or later, they'd search for someone like Sara. Duchamp worried what would be found when they finally discovered their bodies—a lifeless emptiness, or a land thick with last breaths of the dead.

Angie was asleep when he'd left, like she had been for the last six weeks. Every night, he'd sit by her side, holding her hand, hoping she'd wake up. Now, he focused on each exhalation in case it was his last. He wanted to make sure his final echo made it to her, unaltered and pure. A quiet reverberation telling her to stay in the dark, to keep dreaming.

THUGLIT

Flip the Record
by Patrick Cooper

"The gracious existence you deserve," Willie Lynn read aloud from the latest retirement community newsletter. "Gracious existence, this dick."

He tossed the newsletter on the patio table beside him and took a sip of spiked lemonade. He looked up at the sun pounding down between the palm trees. Cursed to himself. Another scorcher. Sweating through his chinos already. Other old-timers preferred the oppressive summer heat. Middle of August and they're walking around in cardigans. Wearing sneakers in the pool.

"Mail call," Henry Galante said, walking up Willie's front steps. "You got a card here." Henry handed him a yellow envelope and took a seat at the table. The patio furniture was sticky with humidity.

Willie thanked him and opened the envelope. It was a birthday card from his son in Jacksonville. He held it close to his face and sighed, "Lookit this shit, man." He held up the card so Henry could see the front.

"It's a kitten with a bow on its head," Henry said. "So what?"

"So what? It's the same goddamn card from the past two years. Kid must've bought a case of the damn things. My own son can't visit my ass on my birthday, and he's sending me the same goddamn card every year."

Henry took a sip of Willie's lemonade. The vodka burned his throat. "Should be proud. Kid buys in bulk. That's smart."

"Don't be drinking my sweet stuff now."

"The vodka's why you're sweating so much, man. And happy birthday."

"Obliged." The men slapped hands over the table.

They talked about the Dolphins' chances this year for a while, Willie getting slowly buzzed on his special lemonade while the sounds of the Bill Evans Trio floated through the screen door. A high-pitched horn sounded as Christian pulled up in a golf cart.

In his mid-30s with teeth as white as the patio furniture, he tossed the two men his aggressively friendly grin. "Hey fellas, how about this sun today, huh?" He shook his head, like he genuinely couldn't believe the weather.

"It's summertime, Sister Christian," Willie said. "What'd you expect the sun to do?"

Willie's jab didn't register with Christian. The grinning fool leaned over the golf cart's steering wheel and said, "Willie, listen, we had another noise complaint last night. A couple people called the office and complained about your music. We can't have you playing loud music, now you know that already."

Willie adjusted the crotch of his pants and sidled up in his chair.

"It was before dark, man," he said. "Don't be givin' me this shit."

"Well, your neighbors hold different hours than you, Willie. You have to respect that."

"Shit, only one way to listen to Charlie Mingus, ya dingus. And that is loud."

"He's got a point, Christian," Henry said. "Mingus ain't no soft-spoken son of a bitch."

It was their mutual love of jazz that first brought Willie and Henry together. Henry was new to the community. His kids felt that they couldn't care for him properly anymore. They were moving on with their own lives. So one afternoon, a cab dropped Henry and his trunk off at the curb of Boca Raton Gracious Homes Retirement Community. Henry took the change in stride. He was used to going from place to place, starting fresh.

After a couple weeks flying solo, Henry heard some Charles Mingus blasting out of Willie Lynn's condo. He walked up the porch and Willie sized him up. He had about forty pounds on Henry. All in the midsection. Henry introduced himself, and they'd been best pals ever since. Two discarded men sitting on the porch, listening to Willie's record collection, watching that God-forsaken sun sink every night.

Christian shrugged and said, "I don't know about that, guys, but Willie, ya gotta keep it down. At all hours. People nap, people go to bed early. Work with us, please."

Willie mumbled to himself, then said, "And tell the delivery boy I need more lemonade mix and peanut butter."

Christian sighed. He shared a look of mutual understanding with Henry.

"Willie, your groceries were delivered yesterday," Christian said, talking slowly. "Check the cabinets. The ones above the sink. It's all up there. I put them away myself."

Henry said to Willie, "Yeah, it's up there, man. C'mon, let's go inside. I wanna get outta this heat anyway."

A dim look came over Willie's face. Breathing through his mouth, he looked up at the palm trees. Henry recognized the look. It meant Willie was getting lost again. He got up from the table and took Willie by the arm. Nudged him and said, "C'mon, pal. Time to flip the record."

Christian mouthed "thank you" to Henry, then zipped away in the golf cart. Henry walked Willie inside. The screen door slapped close behind them. Henry sat Willie down at the kitchen table, Willie still wearing a look of puzzlement on his face. Henry went over to the record player, flipped the vinyl, and dropped the needle. Before Bill Evans played a note, Henry turned the volume down.

The music played and Willie started bobbing his chin gently. The bewilderment departed from his face. Henry watched the transformation. He'd seen it a dozen times before. He smiled and started fixing his friend another drink.

The lemonade mix was in the cabinet above the sink, just like Christian said.

Willie took a few sips and said, "You see that bullshit in the newsletter? About the hike in fees?"

Henry shook his head. "It's some deep, dark bullshit. Five extra grand a year to use the clubhouse and get elite meals during the week. This whole community is a racket, man."

"You know it. This whole grocery delivery service is nearly chewing up my entire fixed income. I can't afford the elite package. And you think that bleach-clean bastard Christian gives a damn? He supposed to be working for us."

"As long as the man gets our rent, you think anyone here gives two shits about how they feed us? That's extra pocket money for those scum suckers."

"I'm eating open-faced peanut butter sandwiches three times a week, you dig? This whole thing…" Willie spread his arms. "…is the prison system dressed up in khaki shorts and Hawaiian shirts. And listen, I was with April two weeks ago."

"April? That pretty young thing?"

"You know it, baby. I was paying my dues, and right behind her was the almighty treasurer's office. Mr. Abbott wasn't there, but his door was wide open, and y'know what?"

"What?"

"The kitty was wide open too. That beautiful safe. And y'know what I saw?"

Henry grunted.

"Enough green to get two lowly motherfuckers like us outta this hellhole and end our lives in peace on some fine Mexican beach."

Henry sat up in his chair. "Man, hold up now. That's not me anymore. Put a freeze on that right now."

Willie smacked his lips and said, "Brotha, the stories you be telling all the time—yeah, that edge don't leave you, playboy. I've seen the clippings. All you gotta do is work your magic, slip your paws in and out the safe, and then we out."

"No way, Willie. I'm not that guy anymore. Uh-unh." Henry's right leg started dancing up and down.

Willie smiled. He knew he had Henry on the ropes. "Yeah, baby. Yeah you is."

"Look where we're living, man. Retirement community. That says it all right there. We're retired. I'm retired." He waved his hand at all the pictures Willie had on the wall. The ones of Willie in Korea. Ones of his wife, Loretta, who passed 15 years ago of lymphoma. The one of Willie holding his son. His old coonhound, Vern, at his side. "We got these memories onna wall and each other, and that's it. And that ain't a bad way to spend the twilight years, my friend."

"It ain't work. Don't think of this like that. You're not coming out of retirement. All it is, is us walking into a room, reaching into a safe, and splitting with more green than Lady Liberty's dress."

Henry rolled his tongue around the inside of his mouth. "I'll need to look at the safe. I can't just waltz in there with a stethoscope and have it open in a minute. It's not like in the movies. It's delicate. It takes time."

"Take all the time you need, baby. I figure we can get it on during the summer social, when everyone's up in the clubhouse doing the jitterbug."

"How we gonna get in the Mr. Abbott's office? No way he leaves it unlocked at night."

"Let me handle that. This April chick is softening up to me. I've still got some of that O.G. charm, know what I'm saying? I can distract her long enough where you go in and unlock one of the windows. Then we come back at night and slide right in."

Henry nodded and looked at his friend. It was foggy up there in old Willie's head, but damned if this didn't kinda make sense. A small seed of excitement started to sprout in his stomach. A familiar feeling he hadn't felt in 30 or so years. Not since the Kansas City job. The one he was still living off of. But even thinking economically, that well was running dry. Henry had budgeted down to peanut butter himself.

"Okay," Henry said. "Say we do this thing. Then what's supposed to happen? We split, they know it was us. Where we gonna stash it anyway?"

"We don't split. Not for a while anyway. We just chill for a while, business as usual. Then in a month or so, we dip outta here. You still have that Chevy Caprice in storage up in Delray?"

"Christ, you really have thought about this."

Willie squinted for a moment. His head shuddered, like he was shaking out the cobwebs, and said, "Yeah, and the thing is, we don't split. We just chill for a while."

Henry sighed and said, "Business as usual?"

"Exactly, baby."

"My passport expired like, twenty years ago."

"Doesn't have to be Mexico, man. I was just talking. We can dip up to Atlanta or even Charleston. Open road with plenty of scratch."

Henry's head bobbed as he looked around Willie's 10x10 kitchen. It was the same layout as his place, the whole condo was. With a bathroom so small he had to leave the door open to pull his pants back up.

He thought about these things and said, "Tell you what, lemme sleep on this." Henry got up from the chair and slapped Willie on the back. "Don't kill that vodka tonight, man. You'll sweat so much in bed, you'll drown in your sleep."

"Shit," Willie laughed. "Now the man's gonna tell me how to drink my liquor."

"I'll talk to you tomorrow," Henry said, stepping out the door. From the porch he called back, "Call me if you need anything."

Willie got up from the table and walked over to the record player. He turned the volume back up. Outside, Henry laughed.

Willie looked up at the picture of his Loretta. He took a sip from his glass and sang to himself, "Loretta up in Heaven, here comes the end of our depression."

Christian called three minutes later and told him to turn the music down, please.

Henry wrestled with his sheets for forty-five minutes, then gave up trying to sleep. That seed was still growing in his guts. He kicked the covers off and got the shoebox out of the closet.

Under the light of the nightstand lamp, he started going through the news clippings.

Kansas City Prudential Bank Robbed! Suspect Still At Large!

Lots about the Kansas City job. A few clippings covered his spree in the mid-sixties—the one that brought him through Arkansas, Oklahoma, and Colorado. Five banks and about a dozen liquor stores along the way and he never took a fall.

Henry smiled to himself. He'd really seen the heartland. And he kinda missed it now, that edge. Sleeping in a different motel every night. Eating at diners, flirting with the waitresses. Getting laid at truck stops. Staying one step ahead of the pigs. Yeah, he missed it.

He always worked alone. Lone wolf, no crew. He did it all clean and never fired his pistol once. Never hurt anyone. Then he'd send some money back home to his sister in Massachusetts and move on to the next town.

The Kansas City job was his big climax. The "whopper," is what he called it when he told Willie the story. He spent the year after KC laying low in Montreal, then he returned to the States and opened a hardware store in Orlando.

He made a little something for himself the straight way for a solid two decades. Had a couple kids with two different women. Then the Home Depot opened two miles away. Henry just didn't stand a chance, and after two years of finishing in the red he hung up his smock and sold the building. It was a bail bonds place now. Go figure.

The trip down memory lane was watering the seed in his stomach. He walked into the kitchen and took the receiver off the wall.

"Huh?" Willie said.

"Yo, Willie, it's me."

"Wh-what time is it?"

"It's about time."

"That mean what I think it means?"

"Let's get it on."

Willie hoisted Henry through the open window and said, "Damn, man. You're heavier than you look."

"Shut up and gimme the flashlight," Henry said. Willie handed him the flashlight and a crowbar they'd stolen from maintenance the night before. If Henry couldn't crack the safe, he'd strong-arm his way in. The old-fashioned way.

He unlocked the front door to the office and let Willie in. Henry worked on the safe while Willie kept an eye out the front window. He heard big band music coming from the clubhouse three hundred yards away. "Tellin' me my music's too loud," he said.

A couple minutes into it, Henry knew he wouldn't be able to crack the box. He'd been out of the game too long and his touch was long gone.

"Yo," Willie whispered. "Best make it quick, man. I think I see headlights comin' round the corner. Probably Christian in his douche-mobile."

Henry cursed and placed the flashlight on the ground, aimed at the safe. It was an older box. Maybe from the late '80s. All those years of wear, Henry figured he could jimmy it open. He strained something fierce, but the box popped open with the most satisfying noise Henry had heard in years.

He shined the light inside. Franklins and Jacksons peered back out at him. With his heart pumping loud in his ears, he took the garbage bag out of his pocket and started tossing the cash inside.

"He still coming?" Henry whispered. Willie didn't answer. Henry looked up to see his friend resting on the windowsill, staring into a corner of the darkened office. "Willie! Yo, Willie! Is he still coming?!"

Willie shook his head and looked up at Henry. "Say what?"

"Is Christian out there, man? What the fuck?"

Christian opened the office door and stepped inside. "Hello?" he said. "Mr. Abbott? Who's in here?"

Henry could see Christian's teeth shining in the dark. He stayed frozen. Kneeling on the floor, bag of money in hand.

"Who is that?" Christian said. He hit the light switch. Willie shielded his eyes from the blast of fluorescents. "Willie? Is that you? What are you doing in here?"

Willie shot a glance at Henry, then said, "Huh? Christian, listen. I just…I woke up here a minute ago. I must've, must've slept walk or something, man. I'm real confused."

Christian took a few more cautious steps into the room. "You woke up here? But how'd you even get in here?"

"I don't feel so hot, man." Willie leaned against the windowsill. "Feeling dizzy."

Christian crossed the room in three big steps and put an arm around him. "Take it easy there, Willie. Sit over here." He motioned for Willie to sit in the desk chair.

Willie punched him in the stomach. Christian keeled over and vomited up the punch he'd had at the social. "Oh God," he said when his stomach was empty. "Oh Christ…"

Henry ran over, the bag of money in one hand and the crowbar in the other. "Willie, what the fuck, man?"

Willie snatched the crowbar out of Henry's hand. He wound up and cracked it off the back of Christian's skull. Christian collapsed in a heap. He made wet moaning sounds. His arm shot out from beneath him and grabbed at Willie's leg. Willie stepped back. Christian's arm stayed outstretched. His hand gnarled into a claw. He went into spasms.

Henry backed up into the wall, watching Christian thrash on the ground.

"The light," Willie said to him. "Kill that fucking light, man!"

Henry switched off the light. Christian continued to spasm there in the dark. It was the worst sound Henry ever heard. After a minute, it was over. Christian let out one last bloody gurgle and died.

"Willie," Henry said. "Willie, man, you fucked us."

"Did you get the money?"

"You fucked us."

"Cut that shit out. Ain't no time to lose it on me here, Henry. You empty the safe?"

Henry held out the garbage bag.

Willie felt his way over in the dark, stepping over Christian, and took the bag. He felt inside and whistled. "Bless those elite meal package pricks, right, my man?"

Willie laughed, and it made Henry want to throw up.

"Now listen to me, Henry. This doesn't change shit. Not a damn thing. We just play it cool and play it stupid when the man comes around asking questions. Ain't no thing, my man."

"But Willie, he didn't do anything. You coulda just kept playing sick. Playing like you was confused how you got here. He was buying it."

"Naw, that's out man. He woulda seen you there any second, bagging the money. We'd be getting hauled away right now if I didn't make a move."

"Christ, Willie." Henry let all the air out of his lungs and breathed in deeply. "Oh Christ."

"Now let's just go back and chill. That's all we can do for now. That's all we gonna do for now."

"What about...what about him? We can't just leave him there, face down in his vomit. It ain't right."

Willie shushed him. A group of people walked by the office window. The social was letting out.

"We gotta go now. You wanna stay here and tuck that asshole into bed for the big sleep, you be my guest. But I'm getting my ass home."

"What about the, about the crowbar. It's got his blood on it for sure. His hair."

"You hide that shit when you get back. I'll stash the cash in a safe place. You don't worry about that. We stick to the plan, right?"

Henry didn't respond.

"Are...you cryin' man?"

"No," Henry said, wiping his dampening eyes with the back of his wrist.

"I said we stick to the plan, right? Right, Henry?"

"Yeah," Henry said. His voice quivered, "Stick to the plan."

"Now you go on. I'll leave a couple minutes after. I'll call you when I get back home. Now go on. All the way live, baby."

Henry did his best to play it cool. Police were everywhere those first few days. Combing every square inch, every blade of grass in the community. Banging on doors and grilling residents over and over. Investigators had personally talked to Henry and Willie four times now, separately and as a pair. Willie did most of the talking when they were together. When he was alone with the brass, Henry recited the rehearsed yarn. He couldn't imagine how Willie had done solo, with his memory fading in and out the way it did.

Investigators kept hitting dead ends. The hunt had been reduced to two detectives.

But they knew. Henry was certain they knew and they were just screwing with his head. Letting him squirm until he couldn't take it anymore and he'd crawl into the back of their police car. In all his life, all the shit he'd done, he'd never hurt anyone. He wasn't built for this type of lie.

Each day, Willie assured him everything was cool. "They don't know shit from shit, man. It's not even on the front page of the paper anymore. There are no more news vans parked outside the gates. No choppers overhead hovering in that warm Boca breeze. And now there ain't nothing to do but be cool and start planning our route north outta this oven. Now let me see it."

"See what?" Henry said.

"The crowbar, man, what do you think I mean? I just wanna know it's safe."

"You know where it is. It's in the trunk. I haven't touched it. It makes me sick just walking past it every day."

"Get outta here with that."

"What about the cash? You never told me where you stashed it."

"It's safe, don't sweat that. It's in the…" The familiar vague look came over Willie. "In the…"

"Jesus Christ," Henry said to himself. Then louder, "Jesus fucking Christ, Willie. You don't remember where you put the cash, do you?"

Willie stood there, in the middle of Henry's kitchen, mouthing words Henry couldn't hear. Finally, Willie said, "In the loose floorboard, under my sound system." He smiled. "Where else would it be, baby?"

"Yeah," Henry said. "Where else. Listen, I was thinking about something. When we split outta here, maybe we should go our separate ways. My sister's still kicking around in Mass. I could stay with her for a while. I could drop you off in Atlanta or wherever on my way up there."

Willie scowled and sat down at the table across from his old friend. "You breaking up with me?"

"It's not like that, man. Just maybe it's best we go our own way for a year or two, then regroup. Once we bounce, they're gonna know it was one of us did Christian."

"We both did Christian."

"You did Christian, Willie. You did."

"That's not how it works. You're just as guilty as I am. That man's blood is on both our hands. Best get comfortable living with that. We been brothers for years, baby. But now that bond's a little different. We connected in a different way now."

The two men stared at each other over the kitchen table. Finally, Henry nodded with acceptance and looked down at the table. He couldn't stand looking at his friend, the killer, anymore. He picked at a ketchup stain. Rubbed his shoulder. It still ached from the strain of popping the safe. He said, "I understand, Willie. It's getting late though. I'm gonna turn in."

Willie got up from the table and said, "I'm a little tired myself. I'll catch you tomorrow. Delivery boy's supposed to bring me some vodka. We can wet our whistle and watch the women's synchronized swimming class at eleven."

Henry knew that Willie just got his groceries delivered yesterday. He had helped Willie put them away.

Another kind of seed began to grow—in his head this time. "Cool," he said. "Call me after the delivery gets there. We'll make a day of it."

Willie smiled. "Always. We're in this together, baby."

Henry set his alarm for 6:00am. Hours before he knew Willie normally woke up. He rolled out of bed, already fully dressed. Sneakers and everything. He went into the kitchen, popped a couple aspirins for his shoulder, and called him.

"Yo, Willie."

"Henry? What is this? Still dark out."

"Man, don't tell me you forgot. You been talking about it all week. We're meeting April and one of her friends down at the shuffleboard court. You said we'd have the courts to ourselves, before everyone got up. Then we'd all have breakfast together then sip vodka lemonades on your porch all afternoon. The perfect day, is what you been calling it. Just us and two fillies."

Henry heard Willie breathing on the other end of the line. He could picture the puzzled look on his face. It gave him a sharp pang of shame. But he kept it moving. "The perfect day, c'mon, Willie. I've been looking forward to this all week."

Willie exhaled and said, "Oh shit, that's today, isn't it?"

"You ain't bailing on me now, are you?"

"Bullshiiiiit. I just musta forgot to set the alarm. I'll be down there in ten. Keep the girls warm for me."

Henry hung up and waited. He stood at his kitchen window, sipping coffee. Six minutes went by, then he saw Willie doing his animated hipster strut past his condo. A bad knee caused him to drag his left foot a little. Henry watched his friend disappear behind the clubhouse, out back to the courts. He left his coffee mug on the counter and picked up the phone again. Called the taxi service. Then he got the stuff and went to work.

Willie watched the sun come up over the palm trees. It was already warm. Sure signs of a scorcher later on. He kicked around the shuffleboard court for thirty minutes. A couple times he forgot why he was there. Some residents came up holding shuffleboard cues. They asked if Willie had the court reserved.

Willie told them he didn't and started the walk back towards his condo. "Fuck is you, Henry?"

The walk took him almost ten minutes. His knee was always the most stubborn first thing in the morning. He stopped to flirt with Mrs. Bowden, former Miss Palm Springs. He thought about stopping at Henry's place to see what the hell was going on, but it was a little out of the way and he had to go to the bathroom.

Mr. Abbott was waiting on Willie's porch with two police officers. The crowbar was wrapped in plastic, sitting on the patio table. Next to it, the bag of money and Henry's shoebox. The one they'd looked through so many times. Laughing and drinking while Henry told his war stories. Sitting at the table, Abbott was reading one of Henry's old clippings. He looked up and saw Willie standing there.

"Good morning, Mr. Lynn," Abbott said. "These detectives would like to talk to you."

Willie shook his head. He rubbed his temple and stared up at the palm trees. He said, "No, see…Henry had the crowbar. The cash was in the…I had the crowbar. Is that right? But Christian…"

The cab dropped Henry off at the auto storage facility in Delray Beach. He tipped the driver enough to keep his mouth shut. The owner of the storage place had been running Henry's Caprice a few times a week to keep it in shape.

Driving up I-95, Henry felt that pang of guilt again. Setting up Willie like that. But what choice did he have. He'd left friends behind before. Pulled them off quick, like duct tape over a bank teller's mouth. Sixty-five years and he'd never taken a fall. It was a record to be proud of.

It was tough leaving behind his shoebox of memories, but that seed growing in his stomach told him to do it. Like an invitation for the police. *Remember me? Kansas City, 1979. I'm out there again. Heading for the heartland.*

"All the way live," Henry said to himself. He popped in a Charles Mingus cassette and turned it up.

Juke
by Kyle Summerall

I can't keep my mind on the six o'clock news knowing what is about to happen. The worry and stress keeps me still on the couch as cut-together videos of panicked schoolkids flash across the screen. Another school shooting in Tupelo and it makes me glad that our kids made way for smoother roads up north. The beer in my hand is warm, and I consider going to the fridge for a cold one, but I can hear Abby in there rattling glasses. I saw her pass a few minutes ago, her sweatpants and baggy shirt traded in for that red lace nightgown she used to wear on special nights. Now I dread seeing the damn thing.

Abby steps out around the doorway, glass half-full in hand, and stands there waiting to catch my attention. I look at her and try to hide the fact that she's ruining my night, and smile. She takes that as her unofficial invite to come on over. She takes the warm can from my sweaty hand and fills the void with a glass of Johnnie Walker Blue, the good stuff. That could only mean she'd drank the rest of the beer in search of enough courage to put that piece of see-through cloth on, and the booze was just a way to make peace for that.

She leans down in front of me and my eyes go right to the scars bubbling up around her shoulders and the blistering red splotches disappearing behind the line of lace running across her chest.

"Want me to get the light?" she asks, already on her way to the switch.

I can't tell her no, so instead I take a slug from the glass, hoping it's enough to dull the edges of barbed wire constricting my insides. The light goes out, and she plops down on the cushion next to me.

It was hard going from two paychecks to one with no help. We'd gone over it months ago. There was no assistance coming. Abby isn't disabled according to the tight-pocketed lawyers. She'd just had a run-in with some bad luck one night and here we are. She can still work, just doesn't want to, doesn't want to have to go out and watch the stares and let her imagination fill her head with all the awful things people around town may or may not say.

Now, she sits around the house waiting for me to come home just so she can do for me and I can't stand it. I can't stand the way I come in after work, aching and dirty, only to feel her start rubbing on me. That sense of her begging me to tell her what I wanted. Some nights I'd come home stone sober and pissed. I'd tell her what I wanted and she'd cry. I've almost stopped going to bed altogether, trading that in for the couch cushions more often than not. That's just the kind of man I've become.

I look at her looking at me, her hand on my leg, and I put mine on the side of her face, the side with the scars. They aren't as uneven as the ones scaling her side, but the skin bumps and craters under my thumb, the flesh unnaturally wet. It reminds me of the sand pits me and Dad used to go out to shoot at whenever he'd done good enough at the casinos to buy another gun. It's that shade of red, almost orange, that gives me that sense of déjà vu.

I see the look in her eyes and the knowledge that I'm a coward rushes to the forefront of my mind like a warning shot. There's no way to get around it. She sees it in me, the selfish pain that has been there since her accident. She can sometimes see past it, but tonight isn't one of those times.

LAST WRITES

She sits back on the cushion, not hard, not to make a show of it, she just sits.

"I'm going to bed, I think," she says.

I want to tell her I'm sorry, use some excuse about my shit day, but in a way, I'd just be lying for her benefit and I'm not sure that'd be the right thing to do either. "Alright," I tell her.

She gets up and heads towards the hallway, then stops. "You goin' out tonight?"

There's still some sun coming through the blinds, throwing thin prison strips on the far wall. "Probably." I'm not left with much of a choice now, I think. My glass is empty and the fridge needs restocking. I remember the cooler on the floorboard of my truck. There has to be a few cans left.

I hear the door close and wait a few minutes before going to stand on the opposite side, listening for all the reminders of why I'm a bad husband. It irritates me more than anything else. She isn't making anything easier on me. Yeah, she spends all her time sitting around, cleaning, calling me four or five times a day while I'm working, just waiting to hear me come through the door. She'd be on me like a slug, wanting and needing things but sometimes, it was the other way around. I'd crawl into bed behind her, grab her, and tell her what she wanted to hear. The sweatpants wouldn't come off all the way and she'd fight to keep my hands away from the uneven blisters, but I didn't care. All I could think about was that I needed this right quick.

I can't hear her anymore and I don't want to go in. I walk back down the dark hallway, grab my keys from the hook and step out into the yard. As soon as the screen door smacks the thin metal frame the oncoming night goes quiet, even those little Feist dogs she keeps in the pen around back don't make a sound, as if the whole damn world is just listening for her squalls too.

I step out into a world divided, Brushy Mountain sitting opposite the setting sun. Here, there is still enough light to move around, but Carpenter is surely dark now, a night brought on early by looming shadows. I get in my truck and start the engine. As I pull out of the gravel driveway, I hear the water sloshing in my cooler. I open the lid and grab one of the beers floating on the melted ice. I dig my phone from my pocket after driving for a few miles with the radio on and dial the only number I have memorized. I let it ring until it goes to voicemail, then try again.

I drive the backroads for a while, catching yellow eyes among the wild marsh buds, letting the cab fill with that wet earth smell that takes me back. Orchids dangle from outreaching limbs flanking the narrow roads heading north, and cattails lick the side of the truck as I go, so much going unseen by the headlights. It reminds me of being eighteen with my friends in the back. It reminds me of being twenty-five with Abby in the passenger seat, her face looking out the window while her hand runs up my thigh. I think about stopping a few times after the beer is gone, secretly aware of my pending destination, but about that time a car would come from nowhere and ride my ass until I sped up. There is no getting away from people anymore.

I continue into Carpenter, taking the same road I take to work every morning, heading to the place where I spend most of my time—Larkin's Bar. It's where I go after work, usually to meet Cathy, but sometimes just to put off going home. I think I would have ended up there either way though, even if Cathy had picked up the phone.

I check the parking lot for Cathy's black Nissan and scan the faces when I get inside for those black curls and mile-long legs. She isn't here, giving me another reason to drink. I take a booth over by the bathrooms and watch the dozen or so people bobbing on the makeshift dance floor while the speakers choke on the blues. No one looks my way and I think it's because they know I belong, as if I'm a fixture, an essential piece to Larkin's. Here, I am among friends who didn't know me and people I could trust not to care enough to tell Abby about Cathy's company. Being a familiar face brings with it a comfort that can only be compared to that of white noise. I bleed into the background and watch everyone else for a while.

She comes in while I'm working on my fourth beer and takes a stool as my eyes take the long walk up and down her legs. The small of her back peeks out of her tight jeans, the bottom of her spine leading right into the spread of her hips. Sometimes when I see a woman, I get so distracted by everything else, I forget to look at the face. Some women are god-blessed with looks everywhere else for this exact reason, but when she turns on her stool, I sigh in relief. I check my phone again and see no missed calls and decide to not let another woman ruin my night.

When I get to the bar, she looks at me then back at the bottle in front of her.

"You want to dance?" I ask.

She gives me a wavering smile that doesn't last. "No thank you. I'm okay."

"Just one dance," I tell her, not wanting to walk back to the booth alone.

"I'm not too good."

"Ain't nobody here good," I tell her, leaning back on my heels.

"I just don't want to dance."

No one comes to a place like this with zero intentions, especially someone looking the way she does. She cuts her eyes sideways as I sit down next to her. "You live around here?"

She takes a drink, "Yeah, for a few years. You?"

"My whole life," I say.

She makes a sucking sound as if she'd pegged me just by a few words. "Yeah, I can see that. A place like this has a way of keeping people."

She's wrong, but I don't bother saying that. The truth was the opposite. Very few people that I came up with stayed after high school. The ones that did, kept on living in a way that hadn't been needed since my dad had been a boy. I look down at my own palms, hard and pale from the cotton I'd picked, feeling her eyes on me. "You can say that about anywhere. Some people have a need to go out looking for something, some don't."

"You can say that about anybody," she says.

I laugh, thinking she would too, but she doesn't. "You waiting for somebody?"

"I think so."

"Then why not come over, sit with me. We'll keep each other company until they get here." She doesn't say yes until I offer to buy the next round.

I try not to overtake the conversation, but do anyway. I'm nervous and I'm sure she can see that. I tell stories I've heard secondhand, messing up the endings and stammering around the good parts. I don't have to wonder why she looks bored. She nods in all the right places and drinks the free beers I get her, indulging me. She keeps looking around and I open my mouth to say something to get her eyes back, but don't. Instead, I decide to tell her about my dad, the only man in four generations to choose going to war over working in the refineries and how it changed him. I tell her how he came back a much quieter man. Sober, he never talked about any of it, but drunk, he'd tell me stories late at night, lit only by the snow moving along the TV left on after midnight.

"Yeah, I think he did it because he didn't want me to end up going. That, or he needed to get it out. He wanted to tell someone. It may have been both."

We add to the kingdom of brown glass as the corners of her mouth travel unworn paths into a smile that has earned its place. When I feel my own smile, guilt hooks me, and I think about Abby and me and how it all becomes sentimental when I start dwelling on it. No matter if I did everything right, sat at home with her every chance I got, when it was all said and done, I'd still be sitting here wishing I'd done more. Regret will find a way just like beer finds its way to room temperature and marriage becomes more about staying together out of fear than love. I wonder what would happen if I went home now, crawled into bed and told her how sorry I was. But what would that change? I'd still wake up tomorrow the same man.

I'm about to get up and get us some more drinks out of habit. When I'd bring Cathy here when she wasn't too busy, she'd keep them coming because she knew the more I drank, the longer I'd last when it came to getting what she wanted.

Before I can get up, she stands, sucking me back into the moment. "I love this song."

I don't have to listen but to a couple of the notes to know Leonard Cohen's "Everybody Knows." Her eyes close as she listens. From here, she almost looks too young to know about that era of music, but I'm looking at her body again.

I stand to meet her, but she talks before I do. "You want to get out of here?"

"Where we going?" I ask, but I'm already following her to the door as Cohen's hushed voice sings; *Everybody knows that you've been faithful, give or take a night or two.*

As we step out into the late September air, free from the dense mugginess that still lingering from summer, she turns away from me. She's looking around again, checking the cars and then searching further out into the trees where all I can see is settled night. "We don't have to go."

She stammers, "No, it's fine. Where are you parked?"

I point at the opposite end. "What about your car?"

She turns and stands at my side, "We'll come back for it."

After I dump the water out and move the ice chest to the bed, we get in my truck and pull out onto the road. "So where we going?" she asks.

"We can get a room."

She shakes her head, "Naw, it ain't like we'll be spending the night together."

I think about that, another similarity I see between her and Cathy. They were both straight to the point, and that's alright with me. "I think I know a place."

"Yeah? It safe?"

I almost tell her how sure I am, seeing as it's where me and Cathy go. "It should be."

The drive is taken in silence as I watch the road being eaten by the tires and she stares out the window. I pull off onto a path that cuts deep into a field of cord grass tall as most men, and we stop just shy of a concrete slab set in the earth. I kill the engine and the headlights, but the open space remains bright under the big-bellied autumn moon and stars.

I look at her as she watches out the window at the fireflies blinking among the deepest blacks between the cords of green moving in the wind.

I think about something Abby told our boy once, back when he was still learning about the world. She'd point out into the field at the winking lights and tell him that *fireflies were nothing more than falling stars trying to find their way back to heaven.* I'd take him out there with a mason jar and a preserves lid we'd cut holes in while he chased him. He'd hold those pieces of heaven in his hands and look at with a light that I couldn't doubt came from the same place. I'd open the jar and he look at me, *Daddy, if we keep them in the jar, they'll never find heaven and they'll die.*

In the wake of time, I think something different than I did back then, everything eventually burns out. That comes from my life in the refineries though, watching the light of coil burn so hot, it's green then blue, and within seconds, goes back to a cold, dead black. They stand out even now, those towers. Their shadows stand out against more shadows, puffing a constant trail of smoke over the tree line that ends up somewhere at the end of the world.

I roll down the windows a bit and let the sounds wash into the cab. Bullfrogs cough, cicadas sing at an unknown frequency off in the trees, and the sound of trains beating down the tracks add a steady rhythm to it all. I sit back in my seat and look at her as she does the same to me. I don't know what to say or where to put my hands so I keep them on the wheel, guilt keeping me still.

She comes at me slow, as if wanting permission—but when she kisses me, it's hard, and it fills my head with the worst kind of desperation. I kiss her back, putting my hands where I want them, waiting for her to tell me to slow down or to break away completely. In my mind, I am the one with everything to lose here. She scoots closer, and then lays back, letting me on top. She bites my earlobes raw and I leave teeth marks on her neck. She's working my pants around my knees when she breaks off.

"You hear that?" she asks.

My hands are in her waistband when she sits up and looks out the back window. "Shit," I hear her say right as she starts wiggling like a wild animal in my arms. She's trying to push me off, but I can't get up with my pants around my knees. She's searching in the floorboard, digging up clothes and throwing them at me when she finds something that isn't hers. I look out of the back glass and see lights curving across the tips of the grass, lighting them up like candles. I get my pants buttoned and am fiddling with my shirt when the car stops behind us.

"You said this place was safe," she says, ducking her head out of the spotlights.

"I thought it was." I think about starting the truck and bolting, but that concrete slab is about six inches high and a foot away from the front tires—no telling what other debris sits unseen. "Look in the glove box."

She opens it and I don't see my pistol.

"Shit, check under your seat."

I reach under mine and she asks, "What am I looking for?"

"My pistol."

"You're gonna shoot 'em?"

I look at her like I want to hit her, and she does what I tell her to. She comes back shaking her head. I try to make out the vehicle, but can't see past the shine of headlights. I pull the latch on the door and push it open.

"What the hell are you doing?" she asks.

I step out in the yellow light and shield my eyes with my arm.

The passenger door on the car opens and I hear, "Get on your knees."

I squint harder, take a few more steps forward, and stop when I hear the gunshot. The crack silences all the other sounds and I jump against the truck when the ruffle of the bullet whizzes through the weeds. There's a sizzle still stirring in the air when the driver's door opens and a large man walks up to me as the wet mud soaks through my jeans. It's strange for there to be so much light, for someone to be so solidly dark. His hand extends towards me, a barrel pointing in my face. I hear the hammer click and I close my eyes.

"Your wallet," is all he says and I give it to him, put it right in his empty hand.

"What else you got in that truck?" he asks.

I feel the truck shake and hear a door slam. I imagine the other guy pulling her out, too.

"Not a damn thing," I hear her say coming around the back end. She has my keys in her hand. "How much he got in there?"

The man unfolds my billfold. "Not much."

"Shit, man," she says, kicking at the ruts in the mud. "Come on then."

LAST WRITES

I hear the gun go off, point blank, and my eyes tighten and teeth grit as I curl into a ball, the world a tunneling echo.

"What the hell you do that for!" she yells at the man.

I hold my breath even after I realize I'm not hit. The truck at my back sinks a bit on that side as the tire deflates.

"I didn't want him following us."

"That's why I took his keys, dipshit." She jingles them between her fingers before tossing them out into the grass. She lays into the big guy some more as they head back to the car.

I lean over and vomit hot beer all over the tire, then choke on the film layering my throat. I hold my hands together, trying to feel solid again.

I ache all over, as if I'd just been in a fight. I remember my phone then, and check my pockets. Not there. I get up and lean into the driver's side door and comb the floorboard before heading over to the passenger's side. I check the seat and glove box, then slide my hand under the seat and pull out my gun. That bitch was smart and had me going the whole way. She must have taken the phone too when I'd gotten out.

I grab a flashlight from the nearly empty toolbox in the camper and head in the direction she'd thrown my keys. It takes me more than an hour, but I find them. I pick my empty wallet out of the mud on my way back to the truck and head home. The ride isn't smooth and the metal rim throws sparks every time the flapping rubber comes off one of the ends, but I take it slow.

The dogs bark the second I pull into the driveway and I can still hear them as I discard my clothes on the living room floor. I look at the couch for a second, but decide to walk to the back of the house. I open the bedroom door and take slow steps to my side of the bed. Pushing away the covers, I slide in next to Abby who has her back to me and reach around her with one arm. I kiss the back of her neck and rub her arm, just enough to get her attention, just enough to let her know that I needed this right quick.

Forever Amber
by Dale T. Phillips

We all know the rules.

Never, ever, fall in love with the help. Don't be a sap, because rules are rules, and anyone who steps out of line doesn't get a second chance. The girls are for hire, that's their job, and you keep things professional at all times. Because in our world, emotion will get you killed.

Tiffany came in and took her seat at the end of the bar. I set her usual in front of her, but she was frowning, looking at her phone screen. She looked up at me.

"Amber didn't check in," she said.

My face showed nothing, but my blood had turned to ice water. "I'll make the call."

I went to the opposite corner of the bar and dialed the number. Someone picked up at the other end, and I explained that one of our girls hadn't checked in after a gig like she was supposed to. Then I hung up like *I* was supposed to. They'd call back. The city was wired, and they'd quickly ascertain if there was a problem.

But I knew.

Deep down, the bottom of my stomach gave way, but I couldn't show a damn thing. Amber had walked the razor's edge for five years, and she knew and followed the rules better than anybody. Not checking in meant only one thing.

And that meant I'd have to do something about it.

If it was as bad as I thought it was, it meant I was a dead man. But I'd take a few people down with me.

The call back came ten minutes later, and I picked up the receiver like it was a spider. The voice on the other end was raspy. "You're not to worry about it," said the voice. "It's not a problem, so forget it."

I hung up, numb inside. A lot of instructions in a few little words. But the meaning was that they didn't know how I felt, didn't know I'd already broken the rules. That was good, for it meant I had a slim chance to stay alive if I was very careful. In the end it really didn't matter, but it's better to live than not, if you can help it.

For the next few hours, I went through the motions—pouring drinks, wiping glasses, lighting cigarettes for patrons—while in my head I was wringing necks and smashing faces. Tiffany's long face showed she knew the score, and our one concession was to drink a toast with Amber's favorite—a twenty-four-year-old scotch. Then Tiffany went home, unable to muster any enthusiasm for work. I continued to run battle plans in my head, a hundred ways of going about this. But all of them led to my bullet-riddled body being dumped in a nearby landfill or construction site.

See, we swim with schools of sharks. No smaller fish can bite a bigger one, because then all the sharks devour the biter. The bigger ones aren't supposed to eat the smaller ones, but it happens sometimes. The big ones can't eat each other, except under extraordinary circumstances. I knew of one time this had happened though, and it had probably led to this night.

There was a system in place, because there was a lot of crazy out there. Guys looking to hire someone like Amber had to give a security code to show that they were sanctioned. If they didn't, the girl would snap their picture and send it out. No one but a crazy would then try anything out of line, and the girls were trained to spot crazy. They didn't have to take unsanctioned gigs, because the regular money was so good, and there was no pressure to do it. They could always turn down some gig that didn't feel right.

Since no picture had been sent, that meant that whoever she'd gone with had given her a sanctioned security code. So someone above had given the all-clear for him to do what he did. It was unorthodox, but the one giving the order would have to be high enough and powerful enough to put this thing through.

I felt in my gut the name of the one person with the kind of juice to make this happen…and would want it to happen. A Council member, one of the highest in the city.

Untouchable.

Seven years ago, Amber had been plucked right out of high school by Big Joe Ranelli, who'd made her his special side lady. Not that she had a great deal of choice in the matter, but she'd made the best of it. Naturally, his roving eye didn't sit well with Donna Ranelli—Big Joe's wife of twenty-two years. She plotted and made deals for two years, and finally Big Joe met his bloody and untimely end—with the grudging approval of The Council. It hadn't helped Joe's cause that his monthly donations had been somewhat short of late. Bella Donna, as she began to style herself, took over Big Joe's seat on The Council—the first woman to do so—after making generous gifts all around. The monthly donations from her territory went up considerably, so all was forgiven and forgotten without further ado.

Amber was a small fish, and Donna hated her, blaming Amber instead of her old goat of a husband. Amber would have disappeared except for a special deal that kept her working for a subsidiary of The Council. Donna probably got a kick out of getting paid every time

Amber lowered herself. And once or twice a year, Donna would send a special gift…a guy who would mess Amber up.

No one knew that I kept a list of each of these guys, and one day there would be a massive accounting, a payback with extra interest. The last thought each of these freaks would ever have is that he'd once made a terrible mistake by hurting a beautiful young woman. I did side work for The Council, and I was good at it, so they would experience pain and horror like they never thought possible.

Yeah, though I knew it was Bella Donna who had done this, I needed confirmation. You don't walk the suicide road until you're sure of who sent you there.

I had found out about Amber's past in the slow stretches at the Bar Sinister, the times she would talk when there was no one else around. I kept things strictly professional between me and the girls, and it was never a problem, no matter how alluring and needy they were.

Amber wasn't like them though, and that was the difference. The rest had backgrounds of absolute horror— tales of rape and abuse and mistreatment to make you wince. It made them hard, made them hate. Not just men, but everybody. Amber had no hate within her. She just had the bad luck to catch the eye of a boss with a vengeful wife. She'd accepted her new role, and served her sentence without complaint. While the other girls blamed everybody else for their lot in life, Amber lacked self-pity, and still believed there were good people in the world.

Poor, sweet, naive kid.

That's what finally broke me, though I never touched her, never spoke to her outside the bar. She thought that if she followed the rules, things would eventually turn out all right. Dreamed that someday she'd take all her savings and go off to find a better life somewhere else. But emotions can get you killed in this business, even when they're someone else's.

For me to ask about Amber's fate was a death sentence. If they got even a whisper that I'd been at all interested, they'd connect what followed with me, and my fate would be sealed. So silence was golden. I needed to leave no trace, or a false trail that couldn't lead back to me. Impossible, of course, but I could try.

So while I waited for the end of the night, I plotted, working out routes and times, figuring angles, making a plan.

A real killer plan.

After I closed the bar, I drove home, checking to see that I wasn't being followed. I always did this as a matter of course, but tonight I was extra careful. I was so alert I was practically vibrating.

With the car parked in the driveway outside, I got some things ready. The little case with the burner phones, their SIM cards kept in a separate, signal-shielded box to prevent my being tracked. A little bottle with some special ingredients. I took a portable toolkit, the kind I used when I wanted someone to talk. In went the small bag of weapons, of course. I put in a stack of bills and some envelopes, because there would be payoffs. Money is the best way of staying alive in this business, money paid to the right people at the right time. And I'd also have to trust some people, something I wasn't real good at, but this time I had no choice. If anybody talked…well, that was that.

I set the automatic program of shadows and lights that would play out and convince anybody watching the house I was still up and around inside until daybreak, when I should be sleeping. Then I slipped through the underground passage to the next yard, beyond the fence. It's a bit much for regular home security, but if you're like me and have actually had people show up at your house to kill you, a good escape route is vital. The passage was why I'd bought the house, and it had saved my life before.

I walked the two blocks to the place where I kept my backup car, the one I used for my other work. There was little traffic this time of night as I drove across town, stopping only at a drive-thru coffee shop that didn't know me, though my purchase wasn't for me. I was soon at the door of a guy I knew, and he answered with a sleepy-eyed annoyance. That disappeared when he saw the fan of bills I held up, along with the coffee.

"Get dressed," I said. "And bring your stuff."

We were in the car a few minutes later. You don't argue with that kind of money, and you sure don't argue when a guy like me shows up on your doorstep at an ungodly hour. I was sure he could use the money. He'd been a sketch artist with the police, and a good one, but they'd switched over to IdentiKits, and his means of extra cash was gone. He was old-school and knew the score. He'd do what I asked and keep his lip buttoned.

The next part was trickier. I drove for a bit, parked and got out, using the first of the burner phones to make a call.

"City Cab," came the voice at the other end.

"It's me, Benny," I said. "I need a favor."

Benny owed me his life, and I was calling in the chit. This whole part was risky, but I had to know. I went on. "Ambassador Hotel tonight, around nine. Blonde, one of our girls, and an out-of-towner." When Amber wasn't working the bar, she worked the Ambassador, only used City Cab, and I knew when she started. Bella Donna wouldn't have hired a local guy for this, even though sanctioned. Amber knew them all.

Benny came back on. "Yeah, Kowalski took it. He's still on shift."

"Have him meet me under the bridge at 57th. Twenty minutes."

"Gotcha. He'll be there."

LAST WRITES

I pulled the SIM card from the phone and dropped it down a storm drain. Then I destroyed the phone. I get these things in bulk, and it just wasn't worth even the remote possibility of ever being traced. The rule was one call and then gone, another habit when you want to stay alive.

I parked near the bridge, left the car running, and got out. Kowalski showed up less than five minutes later, and turned off the cab roof light when still a block away. Bright boy. He pulled up alongside, and I motioned for him to get into my car. We both got in, and I handed him an envelope. He tucked it in his jacket, not bothering to look.

"Whaddya need?"

"Ambassador Hotel tonight, nine-ish. Blonde, one of ours, and an out-of-towner. Describe him."

The guy took a few minutes to give a good description, prompted at times by the sketch artist. All the cabbies could give accounts of a person's looks with just a quick glance, and Kowalski came through like a champ. The guy in back held up his pad, and Kowalski spoke. "Yeah, that's him."

I nodded, and Kowalski got out and returned to his cab. The artist tore off his drawing and slipped it over the seat to land beside me. I looked at it, but didn't recognize the guy, which was what I'd figured. I drove the artist back home, our business concluded.

Next I pointed the car north, to a small airstrip I knew of, little more than a flat field just past the suburbs. Outside of town, I stopped and used the second burner phone to call the pilot. My call woke him, but for what I'd be paying him he wouldn't mind. He wasn't one of the ones our people used, so it would be near-impossible to ever trace him back to me. He'd have the little plane gassed up and ready when I got there.

We flew to Cincinnati, Ohio, even though that wasn't where I needed to be. Only where I needed to be if someone asked. I had to make it as hard as possible to connect any dots. If someone knew certain wheres, they'd figure out certain whos. So I had to disguise the trail, and by not flying direct, I was ghosting.

I napped on the flight, getting what slumber I could. It was going to be a long, tense time before I could get any real rest again, and people had to die first.

We landed without incident, and I told him to be ready to fly us back later in the day. I went to a rental place that was just opening, and used one of my fake IDs to rent a car. I aimed south to Kentucky and hit the gas. On the way, I made a call from yet another phone to a tech geek, a real wizard. I told him I need a jammer, something that would fuzz closed-circuit cameras for a few minutes.

A little past the state line, I stopped and made the exchange. Another envelope of cash for a small box about the size of a pack of cigarettes. He assured me it would work. It better. His life and mine depended on it.

I drove back to Ohio, north and east, to Columbus. In the bowels of the city, I parked outside a large regional hospital and toggled the switch on the jammer. When I entered the hospital, there was a lot of activity. A security guard was standing on a chair, trying to adjust a wall-mounted camera. I knew it wouldn't do him any good.

Up on the fourth floor, I slipped inside a private room. An old man lay in the bed, hooked to a variety of machines and hoses. His skin was sallow, and he looked shriveled and almost gone. But when I stepped beside the bed, he opened his eyes.

"Hello, Carlo," I said.

He smiled, but it was a weak one. A hand came up in a faint gesture. "No way to live," he whispered.

I nodded. "No way at all, for men like us. So I brought you something." I held up the small bottle of the Kentucky bourbon he loved so much. His rheumy old eyes flashed with delight.

"That would kill me," he said.

"It would," I agreed. "I made it special for you, so you won't have to endure this any more."

He made a sound of disgust, a bubble of air coming out from between his lips. "I'm nothing now. And the pain is so bad, you don't know. Everyone from the old days is dead. And so am I. Just being kept around with all this."

"You can go out on your own terms, Carlo. Like a man."

He closed his eyes, but he was smiling. Yeah. When he opened them again to look at me, it seemed like years of aging had fallen away.

"What do you need?"

I held up the sketch I'd had made. "This guy. I'm thinking Vegas, most likely. You know everybody."

"Used to," he said. "Closer."

I moved the sheet in a little, until his eyes adjusted. "Yeah," he said. "Jimmy Snaps. Works for Gaudy."

Anthony Gaudarini. Made sense. There were rumors Bella Donna was having a little side fling with Gaudarini. That's why I'd figured Vegas, but I didn't know Gaudy's crew. With the name and the connection though, I was certain.

"You gonna settle some accounts?" He grinned at me.

"The old way. You'll have plenty of company." I wiped the bottle and pressed it into his hand. "For whenever you want. But if you could wait just one day, that would help a lot. Can you keep it safe and make sure?"

"No problem," he said. "I still got a few tricks up my sleeve."

"Still the man, Carlo."

"Thanks kid. I mean it." It was funny. Nobody had called me kid and lived for a long, long time. I didn't mind it now. I bid him goodbye, leaving him with the final mercy.

Back in the car, I flicked the switch. Their cameras would work just fine now, and there was no trace of my having been there.

I drove back to Cincinnati, and we flew home. I had the car stashed safely away and was back in my place in no time. I showered, dressed, and ate something, and was at work right on time, as usual.

A bit later, a knockout blonde came in. She slid a card across the bar. "I'm with the Agency."

I nodded, hating her on sight. Amber's replacement. "What will you have?"

"Cosmo," she said. "Thanks."

I made her the drink, showing nothing. I didn't want to look at her, and was glad when she got a customer and left. That let me clear my mind for the next stage of my operation.

After work, I went back to the airstrip. This time we flew to Las Vegas, after making a few temporary changes to the registration numbers on the tail of the plane. There was no way and no time to cover up and fly anyplace else that would matter on this trip, so it was do or die. Things would start getting real messy from here on in.

I took out another phone and called a guy who supplied connected people with weapons. I didn't use my name, but gave him a proper code so he wouldn't suspect anything. He met me outside of town, and showed me all the stuff I'd asked for.

"Planning a war?" He snickered, and I shot him with the gun that had the noise suppressor. I wrapped his body in a tarp and tucked it in the trunk of the vehicle.

I didn't know where Jimmy Snaps would hang out, and it wasn't like I could ask around. But I did know that Gaudy ran a particular casino, and I placed myself to watch it. After an hour, one of Gaudy's lieutenants came out, and the valet brought his car around. I followed him when he drove off, but far enough back so he wouldn't pick up on me. He stopped at an all-night liquor store, and when he came out, I grabbed him from behind and pressed the gun with the suppressor against his head.

"This is sanctioned," I lied into his ear, and he relaxed a little. "So you can live through this. Gun first."

He moved his hand very slowly and used two fingers to bring out his piece. I took it from him and tucked it into my belt. I let him go, and stepped back. "We need Jimmy Snaps, and he can't know we're coming."

He wanted to believe me, had to believe this was sanctioned, because he couldn't accept his own death otherwise. His voice was high-pitched, but not in total panic mode, so I figured he'd bought it. "He's got a broad in a place outside of town. Probably there now, still celebrating. Had a big score."

"That big score is why I'm here. He fucked up, bad. Take me there, and you're off the hook."

He nodded, and I kept the gun handy, but not pointed at him. I motioned for him to get behind the wheel. You can't drive and watch someone, so I had to trust that he figured he'd live—and not do anything stupid.

We drove in silence. In a business like this, you didn't ask questions, because the less you knew about certain operations, the better. We got to the place not long after. I looked around. It would work.

"You know I have to put you in the trunk while it happens, right? Should be over in five, though."

He swallowed, but nodded to show he understood. Didn't even bother protesting, because he knew it wouldn't do any good. He figured that a few minutes of discomfort, and he'd be able to move on with his life. We got out, and he opened the trunk. Before he figured out what the shape was that he was seeing, I fired one shot that sounded no louder than a sneeze. He collapsed, and I hoisted him up and rolled him in with the arms dealer.

Good thing it was a big trunk.

I holstered the gun, and retrieved a pair of Tasers—the dart-firing kind. Then I went to find Jimmy Snaps and whoever might be with him.

Half an hour later, we were out in the desert, away from curious eyes. Jimmy lay on the ground moaning, his naked form outlined by the car's headlights.

"Jesus, what'd you do to me?" His voice was whiny. "I hurt all over."

"A little exercise will clear that right up," I replied. I tossed a long-handled spade to clomp into the dirt beside him. "You know the drill. Start digging."

"Hell I will," he said.

"What's her name? The one whose place you were in?"

"Leila? What'd you do with her?"

"Nothing yet. I'm here to give you a good spanking. Do what you're told, you get to learn a valuable lesson, and everyone goes home tonight."

"Like hell."

"Jimmy, if it was a whack, you wouldn't be talking now, would you?"

He thought that over. "What's this about?"

"Your little trip a couple nights ago."

"That was by the book," he said, whining again. "They said it was okay."

"Mm-hmm. You take a picture when you were finished?"

"No…I was told it wasn't necessary."

"You were told wrong, then. Donna wants proof, Jimmy. Got to have the proof."

"I did it, you know I did. Shit, look at my hands, they're still blistered from digging before."

"Rules, I'm afraid. That's what all this is about. Just a little slip, you get a little lesson. They want it to sink in, so

114

that's why we're here. Gaudy spoke for you, hence it's all good. But you need a strong reminder. So get up."

He rose slowly. "I could tell you where she is."

"And you will, Jimmy, and we'll check it out, but now you have to dig. And if she's not where you say she is, someone else will come to you tomorrow night, and that one won't go so well for you. Pick up the shovel."

He picked up the spade and shook his head. "This is bullshit."

"This is business."

He punched the blade into the dirt, pushed down with his foot on the spade, brought up a pile, and flung it off to the side. I watched him work for a bit. "While you work, give me some directions."

He told me where he'd put her, and I made sure I knew where the spot was. He couldn't afford to lie at this point.

Ten minutes went by, and he stopped to wipe sweat from his face with his forearm. "Can I have my shoes, at least? This hurts my feet real bad."

"If it was up to me, I'd say yeah. But it's not."

He muttered something, but got back to digging. He grunted with effort now, and I could tell he was hurting. But he'd be hurting a lot more before this night was out.

He was down about two feet before he stopped, panting. "My hands are bleeding."

"So's my heart, Jimmy."

"Can I have some water?"

"When you get home, you can have all you want. Here in the schoolroom, there are no fountain breaks."

He got back to work, but progress was slow. He kept switching which foot did the pushing, making soft cries. Soon, he didn't even have the breath to curse anymore.

He was down almost as far as his waist now. "Is that good enough?"

"Is that how far down you went for her? You getting sloppy?"

He sighed and resumed digging. I watched the light shine off the sweat on his back, knowing that each stroke was like fire in his hands and feet. In a few minutes, he'd look back on this as the good part of his time with me.

By the time he got deep enough, he was almost to his shoulders, and he just stopped, unable to go on. He had nothing left, and could barely get out of the hole. I made him lie on his belly in the dirt, and secured his bloody hands behind his back with a police-issue zip tie. Then I put my foot on his back and jerked up hard on the bound hands to give his shoulder joints a painful wrench. He cried out.

I brought out my toolkit and opened it up. "So Jimmy, Gaudy had you do this as a favor to Bella Donna, right?"

"Yeah," he croaked.

"Now you're going to tell me exactly what was said, and who said it. And every detail of how you met her and what you did."

"Go to hell," he said. I had to give him credit. Most people would have said anything to please right now, but he still had a tiny piece of the big bad tough guy in him.

I set down the toolkit and went to the trunk. I picked up one of the forms and carried it over and dropped it on the ground next to him. I wanted him to look into her dead eyes and know. And he did. He lost control, sobbing her name.

I set to work, eliciting shrieks of pain. Now he'd know the game was up, but it didn't matter. Within minutes, he was babbling, having spilled everything he'd done to Amber, and most everything else he'd done in life. The desert echoed with screams. I put him through each stage of pain until he was a broken shell of what had once been a man.

When I had every detail, I stood up, panting and sweating myself now. I pulled up on his arms and dropped him facedown into the hole he had dug. I took off my shirt, picked up the spade, and started shoveling the dirt over him. Sounds came from the pit, but they didn't resemble human speech. A few minutes, a little dirt, and Jimmy Snaps was no more.

I drank some water and wiped down. There was still a lot of work to do. Like three other bodies that had to disappear. But not here. Jimmy Snaps was going to be a lonely ghost in a barren spot.

I slept on the plane all the way back from Vegas. After we'd landed, I took the pilot aside. I handed him a couple of bricks of bills. "Take a vacation," I said. "A good long one." It was either that, or I'd have to kill him.

' He nodded. "I've got a friend whose been trying to get me to join him on a gig. Seems like as good a time as any."

Now came the most dangerous part of the whole deal. I laid out all the equipment, and ran over the plan in my head. I knew Donna had eight bodyguards at her place. It was still too early for the housekeeping staff, so I had to go now or never. I made a quick stop to boost a car, then drove it behind a place where the junkies hang out. One of them was still around, not yet having scored. I called him over and told him the deal. I'd give him money if he just did a little thing for me. He was twitchy, but anxious to please, as his need was getting insistent.

I drove to Donna's modest mansion, tucked away for privacy, which suited my needs. I stopped just down the street before reaching the gates. The junkie had specific instructions. All he had to do was wait a few minutes, and roll the car up to the gates when I gave him the signal over the walkie-talkie. The bodyguards would come up to the car, and I told him they'd make him leave.

I didn't tell him the other part.

I jogged around back, along the wall that encircled her estate. When I was at a good spot, I used a nearby tree as a jumping-off point, and got a grip on the top of the wall. I hooked a leg up and slipped over to land on the other side. I pressed the button on the walkie-talkie and told the driver to roll the car up.

A minute later, his nervous voice squawked through. "I'm here, and they're coming over. They're scary-looking, man. Am I gonna be okay?"

My response was to turn off the walkie-talkie and press the switch. The explosion sounded loud in the still morning air, even with a mansion between us.

The two guys in back came out from their spots and ran for the rear door. I shot them both with a little submachine gun with the noise suppressor. As I went in the back way, I switched guns. When they came to see what had happened, I wanted this to look like a coordinated attack from more than one guy, so I was going to use all the weapons.

Two more were just inside, looking toward the front. I plugged them and switched guns again. One guy came down the stairs at a run. I popped him, and headed up the stairs.

A guy's voice came from around the corner. "What the hell was that?"

I came around the corner and got him through the eye. That should have been all of them, but I was alert, just in case. I now had the dart-firing Taser in hand. Bella Donna herself would not go down without a fight, but I wanted her alive for a few minutes. I kicked down the door to what looked like the master bedroom, and two shots hit the frame as I ducked back. I rushed in, hearing another shot, and fired. The Taser dart struck her, and all resistance ceased.

But she'd tagged me. The bullet was in the fleshy part of my upper arm. Good thing she'd just used the tiny bedside gun, and the small-caliber wound wasn't serious. I slapped a quick compress on it to stop the bleeding, and went to where she lay by the bed, her body writhing with spasms. I bound her hands and removed the dart. She lay there unable to do much, but watched me as I took out a bottle and unscrewed the top.

"Who sent you?" Her voice was almost a hiss.

"No one."

"Then why?"

"The woman you had killed."

"That little whore? You can't be serious. She was nothing."

I tipped the bottle, and a few drops fell on her face.

She screamed.

Acid will make you do that.

"This can't be over her," she shrieked. "I'm more important than that."

"Not anymore," I said, and spilled more of the burning acid over her body. She convulsed, her body arching. The next few minutes were pretty bad for her. She cursed and screamed and thrashed, and suffered for what she'd done, and knew why she was suffering.

She was still able to spit out a few final words. "You're a dead man."

"You first," I said. I stood up, and started sloshing the contents of the other container, the one with the accelerant. I thumbed the lighter, and a hungry tongue of flame leapt to life.

"Say hi to Big Joe," I said, but there was no Donna left, just a lifeless sack of meat. The sirens were already coming, and it was time to go.

I ditched the guns in a place where I knew they could be recovered after an anonymous tip. Because I wanted them to be. They would be traced back to the Vegas guy, and I wanted the trail pointing that way.

My setup was that the big sharks had started eating each other. It might play, and would certainly start a feeding frenzy. More people would die, because that's the nature of a gang war. Some would see it as an opportunity to move up, clean house, or settle old scores. There was no other explanation for the massacre that would make sense. And the missing guys in Vegas would add to the mystery, but fit in the scenario I'd set up. Gaudy wouldn't last another twenty-four hours, and I doubted he could talk his way out of this one. He'd know what was coming, and if he was smart, he'd do himself in before they got to him.

Not long after, I was at the bar, moving the bandaged arm as best I could, when Sal came in looking wild-eyed.

"Close up," he said, out of breath. "Shut it down. We got trouble."

I set a shot in front of him, and he dashed it down before going on. "Somebody whacked Bella Donna. We're all on lockdown."

"They need me anywhere?"

"Not now, but stay connected. Looks like Vegas did it, best we can tell. Jesus, what a mess. Right out of the blue. We're all in for it now. You watch yourself."

"You, too. I'll close up and wait for a call."

He left, almost running. There was no one else in at the time, and I looked at the place where Amber used to sit. Later, I'd have time to find her and take her to a decent place where she could rest.

Out of this life, out of this sewer we called a city.

A place where she could lay forever in peace.

All Things Come Around
by William Soldan

It's getting late, and Travis Hayes can't think straight with all the noise. Cody's screams have reached an unbearable pitch by the time the traffic on I-680 slows to a crawl, then stops. An accident. Tractor-trailer jackknifed on the ice. Half a dozen other vehicles lost control trying to avoid collision. A few have gone off the road, partially buried in the snowdrifts along the freeway. Several more have accordioned into one another like a twisted metal centipede. Behind him, impatient motorists lay on their horns and his son shrieks in his car seat. The boy is cutting molars and having a hell of a time of it. No one ever tells you, Travis thinks. No one ever sits you down and prepares you for these things.

"It's okay, buddy." He reaches back, offers Cody the soft, circular teething ring from the diaper bag on the passenger seat. Cody flails, slaps it away. His pudgy little face is ember red and shiny with snot and tears.

Travis checks the traffic ahead of him—still not moving. Three lanes at a standstill, everyone with their blinkers on, trying to merge but getting nowhere. "Come on, come on," he mutters, "move your asses."

The digital display on the dash of the Honda reads 9:07 p.m. They left Travis's mother's place in Columbus at about five-thirty. He wanted to avoid rush hour but hadn't been quick enough. And now this. They should have been home nearly an hour ago.

Cody continues to scream, a wet staccato that makes Travis feel as hopeless as ever.

He finally pulls out the small tube of benzocaine he picked up at the CVS yesterday when the homeopathic teething tablets and clove oil that Emma packed in his overnight bag weren't working. Emma's big on organic food and natural medicine, especially when it comes to their child. Normally, Travis is all for it, and he does his best to respect her wishes. But he refuses to let his son suffer.

"What she doesn't know won't hurt her, right pal?" He squeezes a dab of the benzocaine on the tip of his index finger, then checks the road again. Still no movement.

Travis puts the car in park and turns to Cody. His son's arms flail once more as he reaches toward him, but Travis gets the finger in his mouth, and the screams turn to garbles as Travis works the clear gel into Cody's swollen gums.

"Shhh, it's all—" he begins as Cody's razor sharp incisors clamp down in the groove of Travis's first knuckle. He yells, yanks his hand back. Cody's pitch climbs several octaves, and Travis hears something crackle in his right ear. "No, no, shhh. It's okay, shhh," he says in vain.

He doesn't hear the phone in his coat pocket over the chaos both inside and outside the car, but Travis always keeps his cell set to vibrate when it rings, so he feels it going off. He looks at the caller ID. Emma wondering where they are.

He answers, "Hey, babe." His voice is louder than normal.

"Where are you? Is everything okay? What's wrong with Cody?"

As much as he loves her, he wishes he hadn't answered. She's just one more noise right now. It makes him feel bad to think this way, but sometimes she can be a bit much. And he's got enough on his mind right now.

"There was an accident," he says, but before he can finish she interrupts with a litany of frantic questions.

He waits for a gap and jumps in, "Honey, it's fine. We're fine. A truck went off the road. We're stuck in traffic and waiting to get around it."

She calms down. "But I can hear Cody."

"His gums are just sore," he says.

"Did you try the teething tablets, or the—"

Though he feels a twinge of guilt, he cuts her off and says, "Way ahead of you. In fact, I think he's starting to feel better, actually." This much at least is true. The medicine is working and Cody's fit has begun to subside. "I've got the last bottle of milk ready to go for him, too."

She asks him how much longer he thinks they'll be.

"We're about twenty minutes out," he says. "We'll be home as soon as these damn cars start moving again."

"I hope it's soon. I made tofu for dinner."

"Yum."

"Ha ha, funny man."

Cody's breaths come out in short, quick bursts, but his crying has stopped. Travis opens the cooler compartment of the diaper bag and removes a bottle of milk while Emma continues to talk. When he offers the bottle, Cody takes it.

"Uh-huh," he tells her. "Love you, too, babe. See you soon."

After he hangs up and returns the phone to his pocket, Travis tunes the radio to a classical station and examines the deep red indentation on the knuckle of his index finger where Cody bit him. Didn't break the skin, but hurts like hell.

The clock now reads 9:32 p.m. Cody has finished his bottle in record time and is fighting sleep, a battle he ultimately loses two minutes later when a small opening appears up ahead, just before the pile-up. An exit ramp. Several cars maneuver along the rumble strip in the breakdown lane, and Travis falls in behind them. He follows the ramp's sharp curve as it straightens out into a two-lane residential street. A block farther, he comes to an intersection and stops at a red light.

Relieved to be moving again, but with a head still reeling from Cody's meltdown, he isn't initially aware of where he is. As he sits waiting for the light to change, however, bad memories gather around the car like stray dogs, and Travis suddenly knows all too well.

It's been years since he's been on the South Side, much less on Glenwood. He considers turning right and getting back on the freeway, sitting in traffic as long as it takes. But his temples are still throbbing, and when he imagines Cody waking up, freaking out again, he thinks better of it.

The light turns green. Travis hangs a left.

He's at the bottom end of the avenue, and it's a slow climb on the icy asphalt. He looks out at deserted lots and ruined buildings, nail salon neons and barred windows.

The neighborhood is how he remembers it. A few more vacancies. A few more boarded-up homes. But otherwise the same. Still the type of area many people won't wander around during the day, never mind when the sun goes down. Drive-thrus perch on corners every couple blocks or so, nuclei around which the populace darts and dashes at all hours, buying beer and loose cigarettes. The Foster Theater continues to defy time, dirty yellow bulbs illuminating its wedge-shaped marquee—*Adult Films XXX*—in a stubborn revolt against the World Wide Web.

He spent many days and nights here. Up and down the hill. In and out of condemned houses on shady side streets. Breaden. Delason. Overlook and Evergreen. All the time running.

At another red light, Travis watches bangers in spoke-rimmed Caddies fuel up at the Gas Mart near Princeton, feels the bass from their sound systems in his bones. A deep vibration. Cody stirs, then settles. A faint whistle escapes his nose as he breathes.

LAST WRITES

Not a day has gone by over the last four and a half years that he hasn't been reminded of just how lucky he is. To have Emma and Cody. To have placed one unsure foot in front of the other until, at last, he was no longer a part of that world. This world.

Emma never knew the other Travis, and never will if he can help it. He was a year out of treatment when he met her at the health food store where she works. He came in looking for something to help him sleep. She was out of his league but helpful, and she laughed at one of his unfunny jokes. He'd researched various supplements online—milk thistle, 5-hydroxytryptophan, melatonin, GABA, passion flower tea—things shown to promote detoxification, relaxation, and elevated mood. After a few weeks of visiting the store, he asked her out and she said yes. He took it for a fluke, but she went out with him a second time, a third. By the time it occurred to him that he hadn't thought about his old life in a long while, they'd been together for going on a year and had a kid on the way. It seemed impossible, and he began to wonder when he'd wake up from it all. He still wonders.

"Things sure turned out for the better, huh, buddy?" he says, and glances in the rearview to check on the boy, whose head is lolled to the side like a fragile flower. He passes beneath one of the sodium street lamps, and Travis notices a glimmer of spittle running from the corner of Cody's mouth. Travis smiles.

The weather is frigid, just above freezing, so besides the gas station, there are few people on the streets. Two dark shapes lurk to Travis's right in the doorway of the old Park Hotel, smoking cigarettes and giving him the stink eye. One steps out from the shadowy alcove and moves toward the passenger window, hinging at the waist to look inside. Travis feels that feeling again, the one that always preceded a terrible decision. Tightening throughout his body. Sweaty palms and rising pulse.

The light changes, and Travis thinks, *Not tonight, fellas.*

125

The tires of his Honda spin on the slick blacktop before they bite. As he passes a Family Dollar with its metal security doors rolled down and a fenced-in car lot, he looks back and sees the guy raise his arms, as if to say, What the fuck? A moment later, the man drops his hands and turns back to his dark shelter as Travis crests a hump in the road.

Since first turning onto the avenue, his gut has been tight knot of nerves. The closer he gets to being out of the neighborhood, however, the better he feels. His heart rate returns to its normal cadence, and the knot begins to loosen.

He's about to pat himself on the back, tell himself 'Good job,' but as the street curves past a block of dilapidated brick duplexes and a Baptist church, that old voice returns. The one that used to bark at him from the depths whenever he was attempting to act in his own best interest. The one that visited him every night as he sweated it out in County, during the late hours in the halfway house, and as he white-knuckled it through meetings that first year. One negative affirmation after another.

Don't fool yourself, kid. It's just the same resolution all these miserable fuckers make when they hear the gavel fall. When they run out of cash and run out of credit. Next it's vow to walk the righteous path, find Jesus. All that happy shit. Give it up, kid. You can pretend, but people don't change.

He doesn't get into the usual dialogue with it, doesn't argue and doesn't deny, just turns up the radio a few clicks and drives a little faster.

A hard bend in the road and he's no longer on the Avenue but on Midlothian Boulevard. The dividing line between where people want to be and where they don't. Ahead, the luminous sign of Popeyes Chicken & Biscuits springs into view.

He's more or less succeeded in embracing healthy living, but now that his gut has untangled, he's hungry, and the rationalization comes easy: He's been a good boy—a little fried food won't kill him.

See, you're still the same.

The sign grows larger as he gets closer, closer to being farther from that world again.

The same as you always were.

He turns into the Popeyes parking lot.

The same as you'll always be.

"The truck stop is a far cry from the farmer's market," Emma said the first time she and Travis went away for the weekend.

They'd stopped to get gas and stretch their legs. She had packed a cooler with healthy snacks—fruits, vegetables, hummus, bottles of spring water. When Travis came out of the store with a bag of Doritos and a Monster energy drink, Emma started in with that tone she adopts when "educating" people about the horrors of the food industry. "That stuff is packed with preservatives and artificial colors," she told him. "If you can't pronounce the ingredients, it's pretty much poison."

He's since memorized her rhetoric, parroted from Netflix documentaries and the *Huffington Post*.

Trans fats and processed sugar are the real terrorists in this country.

Margarine is only one molecule away from plastic.

Wheat has us hooked like heroin.

Travis often wants to laugh when she goes on a rant. He wants to tell her that we also share roughly eighty percent of our genetic makeup with cows, that everything is only one molecule away from something else, and that when it comes to comparing wheat to heroin, she hasn't got a damn clue. But he doesn't. He's afraid a certain door will open, that certain truths might step through. So he chants his mantra instead: What she doesn't know won't hurt her.

So far, it's been enough.

The tinny voice coming through the speaker reads back his order, and Travis pulls up to the window. A pretty black girl wearing a visor and headset takes his money, tells him they just dropped a fresh batch of chicken and it's going to be a few minutes. He can see that she's pregnant, and when she spots Cody sleeping in the car seat, she makes small talk.

"Aw, he's cute," she says. "How old?"

"Just about a year and a half," he says, then nods toward her bump. "How far along?"

"I could pop before your order's up." She laughs as another car pulls up to the speaker behind him, then closes the pick-up window and begins talking into the mouthpiece of her headset.

A few minutes turn into a few more, and the girl pokes her head back out the window, says it's going to be a bit longer. She apologizes and tells him he can pull up, that someone will bring it out to him when it's ready.

"I'll try to toss in a little something extra," she says, and smiles toward Cody again. "Take care of that little cutie-pie."

He smiles, then pulls out of line and into a parking spot.

It soon becomes apparent to Travis that the discrepancy between the concept of "fast" food and the actual speed with which it's delivered is yet another reason he doesn't miss eating the stuff. He looks at the car's digital clock. Thirteen minutes. He's been waiting for thirteen minutes. It's been just over half an hour since he got off the phone with Emma. They should have been home by now. She'll be calling again soon.

LAST WRITES

Part of him thinks, *Screw it, just go*. But he's paid for it, so now he's committed, invested in the situation. All in.

The dilemma now is whether to go in and get his food or go in and get his money back. He figures he'll decide by the time he gets to the counter.

But then there's the issue of Cody. He reaches back and brushes the boy's shaggy bangs out of his face. Should he wake him up after the ordeal of getting him calmed down? He looks at the restaurant. The register is within view. He thinks, *Don't even.* Then, *It won't take but a minute.*

He tucks Cody's baby blanket around him and considers leaving the car running with the heat on.

What if someone jumps in and drives off?

Won't happen.

But it could.

Come on.

Inside, the smells of fryer grease and spices make him both queasy and ravenous. But ravenous wins, and he decides that he still wants the food. He walks to the counter. When the guy in the batter-stained polo shirt hands him his bag of chicken and fries, Travis's stomach begins to grumble and flip, similar to the way it would before he used to shoot up or hit the pipe. The thought unsettles him, but only for a moment before someone says his name.

"Yo, Travis."

He's halfway out the door and freezes. It's finally happened. He's always known he might eventually cross paths with someone he used to run with, or worse yet, someone he burned. Eventually, all things come around. As he turns toward the voice, puts a face to it, he discovers it's the latter.

"Where you been?" The guy stands up from a table where three other guys remain seated and eating. His words come out slightly muddled as he speaks through the sparkle of his platinum grill. "I been lookin' for you for a long time."

His name is Q. One among many of Travis's dealers before everything changed. As with most of the guys from whom Travis scored, Q let him open up a line of credit because Travis always made good and was a steady customer. But when Travis was ordered to six months in rehab in lieu of jail time for a botched robbery, he got it in his head to go out in style. His initial plan was to rip off every dealer that would front him. Cut ties. A little insurance policy for when he got out, something to guarantee he wouldn't come back around. But Q was the only one he could track down that would let him owe. Travis took him for a bundle of dope and then some.

He plays it cool. "Q, what's up, man? I've been plannin' on hittin' you up."

"Uh-huh." He steps closer to Travis, his hands in the pockets of his puffy coat.

"Things have just been crazy lately. You hear I got locked up?"

Q cocks an incredulous eye. "Yeah?"

"Right after I saw you last. I just got out a few months back. They got me checking in and pissing in a cup every week."

"You bit down in Belmont?"

Travis has never done time in the joint. His minor offenses have never landed him past County. But he's known enough guys who have gone down for long stretches in places like Lucasville and Mansfield and Belmont to talk the talk. Still, he hopes this conversation ends sooner than later.

"Yeah, it's another world down there, man," Travis says.

Q smiles and his teeth glint like foil. "Fuckin' gladiator school," he says. "You got your stripes now."

Travis thinks for a moment that this might be as far as it goes, but he knows better. There is no statute of limitations on the street. He just wonders how long Q wants to catch up beforehand.

As it happens, not long.

Q's grin levels out. "So you got me?"

Travis is coiled inside like a rusty spring. He glances out at the car and sees the top of Cody's head, thinks of running. Bad idea. Even if he could make it to the car before Q or one of the other three guys caught him in the parking lot, what then? Q has put holes in people, at least three bodies from what Travis has heard.

You fucked up, kid.

He's got no choice but to make good. He does a quick mental calculation. Two grand and change in the bank. About ninety bucks in his wallet. Emma will want to know where the money went, but he'll worry about that later.

"We can head over there real quick." Travis points with his clutched bag of food toward the ATM at the Home Savings and Loan across the street.

"All right," Q says, and nods. He leans in to whisper something to his boys. They wipe their greasy mouths and stand up.

When they get outside, Travis starts walking toward his car.

"Nope," Q says as his boys walk up on Travis and grab his arms. "You ridin' over with us."

The coil inside him continues to tighten. "Come on, Q, my kid's in the car, man. I can't just leave him in there."

"Since when you got a kid?"

"Since just before I went downstate."

"How old?"

"About eighteen months." He's already said it before he realizes his mistake.

It's been over four years since they've seen each other, and right now Q's face appears to be working out the math. After a moment, he seems to settle on a number, realizes things don't add up.

"That means you was still on the street for a long time before you went to the joint."

Caught in the lie, Travis goes blank.

"Shit, it don't matter," Q says. He removes a hand from his coat pocket and gestures toward the car. "You left him in there already."

"At least let me check on him first."

Q nods to go ahead, and his boys release Travis's arms.

He opens the back door and leans in. Cody hasn't budged. He kisses the top of his son's head, checks to make sure he's covered and warm. "I'll be right back, buddy," he says. Cody lets out a soft sigh. Travis thinks, *I'm so sorry*, then shuts the door and bites back the tears.

They get into the Escalade that's parked a few spots down. The drive across the street seems to stretch out forever. Travis feels caged, wedged between two of them in the backseat. No one speaks.

When they pull up beside the ATM and let him out, Q gets out with him. He stands with his hands still sunk into the pockets of his puffy coat. Travis puts his bank card into the machine.

At the fifty-cents-on-the-dollar rate Q always charged him on his fronts, the three hundred Travis had been into him for automatically doubled.

"So it's six, right?" Travis says before punching in the numbers.

"Plus interest."

Shit. He hasn't accounted for what Q might tack on for him being MIA all this time. In the corporate world it's called "delinquency." In Q's world it's called "lucky you're still breathing."

"Yeah," Travis says. "So where's that put me?"

Q takes a moment to consider it. "I always liked you Travis. Let's make it a straight G and we good."

Travis feels himself wince. As good of a liar as he can be, he'll never be able to explain such a large withdrawal to Emma. He'll have to come clean with her.

"I can do that," Travis says.

As he starts typing in the amount, Q says, "You look like you got your shit together, Trav. Joint musta' done you some good...if you went to the joint."

Travis is about to respond when the words appear on the screen: CANNOT EXCEED $300 WITHDRAWAL FROM ATM IN 24-HOUR PERIOD.

His heart seizes in his chest. His stomach jumps and falls flat.

No. No no no.

He turns to Q. "It won't let me take out more than three hundred. I have to go into the bank. And it's closed till the morning."

"Travis, Travis, that's no good." Q's hand moves in his pocket, and Travis thinks, *It's all over.*

His thoughts grope one another, trying to construct a solution, a way out of this. He's about gives up when he remembers—a kid named Mickey. Young. New to it and going hard like he had something to prove. Lifted his old man's card. They ran into the same problem and discovered by sheer chance they could go to multiple ATMs and take out more money. They skated around town hitting different machines. Three days and three grand later, the account was frozen. Fun while it lasted.

"Wait, wait," Travis says. "I can hit a few more ATMs and get the rest. I've done it before."

Q looks at him with that cocked, incredulous eye, then motions for Travis to get in the truck.

There are two other banks and a corner store within eyeshot of Popeyes. As they drive him to each one, Travis feels his phone blowing up in his pocket. Emma. He ignores it and keeps his eyes on the Honda. He pictures Cody inside and prays he's still asleep.

He pays Q his thousand dollars, and they drive him back to his car. Only when they get there, they keep going. Toward the back of the restaurant. They've barely said a word the entire time, which unsettles him. They stop next to the Dumpster. This part of the lot is in the building's shadow, and he can no longer see the Honda. They let him out.

"Look, Q," Travis says, standing outside the SUV's passenger window, still holding his bag of chicken and fries. "I never meant to do you like that. I was just out of commission, you know?"

"We cool," Q says. He smiles again, flashing platinum.

Travis nods and turns to walk back. He gets within sight of the car, then hears, "Yo, Travis."

He turns around and sees the pistol in Q's hand. Smile gone.

Everything stops.

Travis steps outside himself, watches from beside himself yet somehow still inside himself as the Glock chamber glides and snaps back and the muzzle blooming spits whipcracks of light—and the him he stepped out of takes them one-two sledgehammers and a wrecking ball in a chest flood of molten feeling…

Smell of gunpowder and scorched rubber.

Taillights.

Ears ringing and body…

…falling.

The cold pavement reaches through his back and steals his breath. Sounds swim through his head—voices, distant cars. Is that Cody? He can't move his body. He thinks again:

LAST WRITES

You fucked up, kid.

Thinks, *It won't take but a minute.* Thinks, *I'm so sorry.* He sees the car, a blur with windows of reflected light. He moves his lips to speak, but only gasps. There's no one there to hear him, anyway. In the dark. His pounding heart is the only sound now. He turns his head, watches his breath rise like smoke. A moment or a lifetime, he doesn't know which, and the stars begin to come unglued. No, not stars, he thinks as they melt against his face. Snow.

He sees this all before returning to himself, no longer both inside and outside, but only inside himself. He stares into the barrel of the gun, several feet away yet gaping with its cold finality. He has time, Q has given him that much. Time to think of all he'll miss, of all he wishes he would have said and done and done differently. So many things, differently.

He closes his eyes and sees Cody's face.

Please forgive me.

Then there's the dry-fire click of an empty chamber. Travis opens his eyes.

Q still has the gun raised, but again he's smiling. A chrome flicker. "Bang," he says, and he and his boys begin to laugh. When the laughing stops, Q says, "You," and wags the Glock at him. "You better remember this."

The window of the Escalade goes up, and they drive off.

On the way back to the car, Travis stops, bends over and dry heaves, but nothing comes out. He realizes he's still clutching the bag of food and drops it on the ground behind the car.

When he opens the passenger side rear door to check on Cody, the boy is awake and looking up at him, his chin spittle-slick. He looks happy. Travis unbuckles him, holds him, presses his numb face against his son's warm one, kisses him on the eyes. Cody says, "Da-dee," and pats Travis on the cheek with his soft little hand. "Da-dee da-dee." It's not the first time Cody has spoken, but it could be for all it makes him feel.

When his phone goes off again, he hesitates before answering.

Don't say anything.

What about the money? I'll have to explain.

You'll think of something.

He thumbs the screen. He hears Emma's voice but not her words.

You'll think of something.

"It's all over now," he says, "We're on our way."

He hangs up and puts Cody back in his car seat. As he backs the car out of the parking spot, he feels the tires crunch over the greasy sack of chicken and fries. Driving out of the lot he sees it there in the side view mirror, and for a brief moment, he sees himself lying on the cold ground beside it.

Prowl
by James Queally

Waking up to the sound of Vanessa's voice should have been a good thing.

The leggy divorcee with the endless black hair and the penchant for stocking craft beer inside her West Hollywood loft had been a revelation. A high-water mark in my relentless pursuit of women over forty.

Now, if we were at her place, ten feet from the balcony that overlooked Sunset where we liked to fuck in plain view of her neighbors, things would have been fine.

But as I struggled to wake up, rolling off my barely inflated air mattress and onto the pile of Brillo pads my landlord called a carpet, I realized things were anything but fine.

I heard the footsteps. Her voice getting closer. Vanessa wasn't supposed to know where I lived.

I tried to move, stumbling in the sluggish Frankenstein's monster gait that comes with disturbed sleep, when I caught sight of the gleaming emerald. It was seated inside a size-seven ring, perched atop my wallet on the nightstand. She called my name again, her voice high-pitched and panicked and angry and—fuck, she knew I took the ring.

"Lonnie!" she shouted again. I looked around the bedroom to find it empty, but the apartment wasn't that big. She was somewhere between me and the door.

I heard footsteps, heavy ones that definitely carried more weight than her bird-like frame.

Great, she'd brought a friend. Now I needed to break out of my own fucking apartment.

The place was laid out railroad-style. The front door led into a living room, then a tiny hallway led to the kitchenette, a quick offshoot to a pisser, then back to my bedroom, and then nowhere. Which was a problem. To get out, I'd have to go through a cougar who probably knew I'd stolen from her and a goon who probably thought touching me inappropriately would get her to touch him inappropriately.

I took a quick scan of my room, stumbling into my pants and snatching up the ring as I searched for the things I'd need to run with. I frantically unplugged my laptop and jammed it into my backpack, then turned to the pile of shoeboxes containing the comic books that were my only other lasting possessions. I stuffed a fistful of issues into the knapsack, hoping I'd have time to get the rest later.

I moved into the hall. They hadn't made it to the back yet, which meant I had just enough room to maneuver. There was a clear path from me to the bathroom, so I took it, turned the shower on and dove back to my bedroom, hoping the kind of guy Vanessa could rope into a strongarm at 8 a.m. was dumb enough to follow the sound.

I peered through the doorway and found a massive Armenian with a linebacker build and the kind of face that would cause a hooker to charge double. Vanessa was at the edge of the hall, somehow looking above-average at the ungodly hour.

She shrieked when I appeared, but not fast enough for the goon to do anything about me running full speed, kicking him in the dick and shoving him into the scalding hot shower water. I'm not above dick kicks. After all, when you wake up on the run from the divorcee you robbed after three nights of letting her tie you up because it got her off—well, you're not really above anything.

The goon had one hand protecting his nether regions as he tried to climb out of the shower, which was a bad move, because it let me use his free arm to tug him head first into the marble sink.

Satisfied I wouldn't have any ribs broken before breakfast, I stepped out of the bathroom to find Vanessa's face snarled up in an ugly cry-scream combination.

"I'm sorry. Things just aren't working out," I said.

"You fucking robbed me!" she shouted.

"You broke into my house and forced me to kick a guy in the balls...we're just not on the same page anymore," I said, pushing past her toward the door. "I'll miss you, Vanessa."

I mean, I would. Vanessa had been a great lay and an even better source of income. I'd taken a couple hundred dollars in cash, a half bottle of painkillers siphoned over time and a nice amount of DVDs off her before I'd gotten greedy and snatched something she would notice.

But now she knew where I lived and what I was about. Which meant I needed a new place, a new cash cow, a new line of survival.

I needed a date.

Jay and I had played in terrible punk bands together growing up in South Jersey, before we both moved to L.A. We had hopes of living somewhere with cultural relevance beyond the Wawa convenience store chain. We'd lived together for a time here, and remained close even after his screenwriting career took off and he got engaged to a woman who seemed biologically predisposed to hating me.

So when I snaked my way through the lunch crowd at the downtown Grand Central Market and tapped him on the shoulder, I wasn't expecting him to cock back a punch to throw.

"You stole my fucking Xbox!" he shouted.

Was hoping he wouldn't figure that out…

Jay stood there for a minute, face twisted in fury, arm still tensed as the mosh pit of people waiting in line at the various food stands looked on. Jay was the kind of guy who'd rather die than make a scene, so he lowered his arm when he noticed our reunion had an audience.

"Can we talk?" I asked.

"Can I get my Xbox back?"

"You know the answer to that question," I replied. "C'mon, I'm in some trouble. You know how it goes."

"I know I'm the last person around who will tolerate your shit, and I know you robbed me anyway, so what the hell are we even gonna talk about?"

"Listen man, I'm just at a low point," I said.

"Your entire life is a low point, Lonnie," he replied. "You're almost thirty. You can't live like this."

"Well, not exactly like this," I said. "Can't roll cougars once I stop being a cub."

Jay looked at me like he was reconsidering the whole 'punching me in public' concept.

He started walking away, but I followed him up a small staircase toward the rows of dirty metal tables in the back of the market. Jay pulled out his iPhone and plopped into a chair, not bothering to look me in the eye, but probably sure he wasn't going to be able to get rid of me either.

"Talk," he said.

"I almost got caught today."

"Lonnie…I'm not hiding you from the cops."

"No, no cops. Not yet anyway," I replied. "Woman I'd been seeing—"

"You mean bleeding dry."

"Like I said, seeing…well, she figured out my habit of borrowing things that weren't mine. Found my apartment.

Which means I can't go back there. And I'm gonna need a new source of income quick to find a new place so I was wondering if you could—"

"Stop," he said.

"I'm not asking you to loan me anything just—"

"Stop. Just stop Lonnie," he said. "How long have we been out here now? Three, four years? I know you've been busy fucking up since then, but the roles were reversed when we started this. You were good, when you actually worked. When's the last time you wrote?"

It had been a while. A couple of months easily. It was hard to get inspired when you spent each month agonizing over how many thefts disguised as one-night stands you needed to make the rent check.

"I thought so," he said, registering my silence as a response. "You know there comes a point where trying to be something turns into failing to be something, right?"

"Jay, I came to you looking for help, not a lecture," I said. "I just need a break."

Jay smiled, like he'd been waiting for me to say that.

"I would have told you about this sooner, but then I figured out you broke into my apartment," he replied. "But I actually do have something for you. Not that you deserve it."

He stopped talking. My tongue was probably halfway to wagging at that point. I owed him the miniscule begging—I had robbed him after all—so I placated him with a little "C'mon, c'mon tell me," even though we both knew my humility was horseshit.

"I met a showrunner over at the CW a few months ago. She works on the superhero stuff, the kind of stuff you used to do," he said. "Her name's Linda Reyes. She's always on the hunt for new talent, has sort of a reputation for discovering writers, and I slipped her some of your old shorts. She's interested in a meeting. She's also recently divorced."

"Are you getting me a meeting or a mark, Jay?" I asked.

"That's up to you," he replied.

I did some of my best thinking while my head was between a woman's legs.

The lady in question, a hospital executive named Doreen, wasn't much of a talker during sex. I think she got hot over the fact that I knew what she wanted and did it without asking. She got hers, and I got time to review my perilous financial situation.

If I was going to treat Jay's associate as a meeting and not a mark, then other people were going to have to cover the bills. I did some quick math as my tongue made slow work of Doreen, trying to figure out exactly how much it would take to keep me from robbing my potential future employer.

A new place was going to require at least $1,500 down between first month's rent and a security deposit. I'd need another couple hundred for food, even if I kept my meals to taco trucks and Tommy's burgers. It would take at least $2,000 to stay off the street, and pawning Vanessa's ring wasn't an option, since she might have reported it stolen.

I opened my eyes, peering out over Doreen's thighs to scan her bedroom and figure out what she might not miss and what its retail value was. She let out a little yelp and twitched, looked at me like I fucked up.

"Hey Danny," she said, causing me to pause for a second when she used one of the half-dozen fake names I gave out with the regulars. Sometimes even I forgot who I was.

"Less teeth," she commanded, looking down on me, her mouth dripping with the satisfaction of looking down on someone.

LAST WRITES

I did what I was expected to and felt Doreen's legs tighten around me as I brought her where she needed to be. The next part of her game was the denial, the taunt, the wait. She'd pull away from me, make some kind of alluring pose, then sneak outside for a cigarette before coming back to finish me off. She had no idea that my time alone in her bedroom was far more valuable than the half-assed blowjob she'd give when she came back.

Doreen lived in a downtown loft, one of those gentrified spots between City Hall and Chinatown, and they frowned on nicotine. She'd need to descend four flights, slip outside, and walk fifty feet from the entrance before she could legally light up. I had about eight minutes.

I waited for the *ding* of the elevator to make sure she was gone, then started scouring the nightstands around her bed and dresser for signs of neglect. A coating of dust on a jewelry box, a collection of coins in front of a drawer that would have gone flying if she opened it regularly, an item tucked behind wrinkled dresses that hadn't been ironed because they'd fallen out of rotation. Anything of value tucked away in a place she wouldn't check anytime soon.

I wasted a few seconds hunting in the closet before I noticed the tri-folded mirror at the center of the dresser, the one Doreen liked to stare into when she was on top. There was a cluster of smaller wooden boxes and folded laundry flanking each side, a blockade that seemed to extend beyond the mirror's edges and toward the wall. I moved a pile of folded stockings to reveal a whiskey-brown jewelry box that was coated with the contents of a vacuum bag. I wiped away the dust to find its key latch was just for decoration, and smiled when I looked at the array of watches inside.

They had to be worth a couple hundred, a nice chunk of the security deposit for that hypothetical apartment. I dipped the watches into my crumpled jeans and moved back toward the bed, waiting for Doreen to reward my patience.

My celebration was interrupted by the sound of the front door swinging open, and the stomp of dress shoes that couldn't belong to Doreen. Unless she'd walked outside, received a direct order from God to quit smoking and then sprinted back upstairs, I was pretty sure this meant I was about to meet Geoff.

Geoff who had no neck in the pictures I'd seen.

Geoff who was supposed to be on a four-day weekend in Vegas with his college buddies.

Geoff whose wife I'd been fucking and stealing from.

I darted for the bathroom, which was quickly becoming my chosen method of escape from cougar-theft-related beatdowns, and hoped Geoff had stopped to take a piss somewhere on his way home. Doreen's apartment was thankfully much nicer than mine, which meant the bathroom had two entrances, one to the hallway into the living room, the other back to the bed.

With my head against the door, I listened as he moved around. A refrigerator opened. A TV buzzed to life. There seemed to be no rush to my restroom hideaway. I patted down my jeans, made sure I had my wallet and the pilfered watches, then realized I was barefoot and shirtless. I couldn't move back to the bedroom to reclaim my shirt and socks, not yet at least. And where were my shoes?

"The fuck?" Geoff snarled.

Oh yeah, the living room.

I searched the bathroom for weapons, which was the second dumbest fucking thought I'd ever had, not far behind "I should move to Los Angeles." The bright pink loofah, monogrammed robes and orange face wash weren't going to do much against Geoff's ape fists.

Thankfully, the door groaned a second time, announcing Doreen's return.

"These aren't Bobby's shoes," Geoff shouted.

"Geoff?" she asked. "What are you doing home?"

"Bobby's a size 12," he continued. "Who the fuck is in my apartment?"

I had questions. Ignoring any instinct of self-preservation, I slowly turned the knob and opened the door just wide enough to take a peek.

"We had a goddamn agreement Doreen. You wanna fuck the boys we swing with? Fine. But no randoms. Goddamnit, I don't want to have to get tested again. You know how nervous that makes me."

"Oh, like I'm not going to have to see the gyno after another one of your Vegas weekends Geoff? How many? Two? Three?" she fired back. "I guess they don't laugh about your armpit fetish if you pay them enough."

Between Vanessa's ability to send a heavy to my apartment and my discovery of the phrase 'armpit fetish,' I started to wonder why I always picked such overdramatic marks. I would have laughed, but things stopped being funny when Geoff ruined Doreen with a stiff right hand.

"Laugh it up bitch," he said, taking his belt off.

"Oh shit," I said out loud, then stumbled back from the door as I realized I'd actually said that out loud.

"So you do have a friend here," Geoff said.

I scanned the bathroom for weapons again, a mix of urgency and panic leading me to a pair of hairspray cans and little else.

I opened fire as soon as the door swung, dousing Geoff's face with enough product to turn a Mohawk into a deadly weapon. He groaned in disgust and put his hands out to try and stop the mist before he banked left and tripped over the lip of the bathtub, his head landing along the sliding door track.

I grabbed the handle without thinking and swung it right, smashing the edge into his neck, forcing him into an emphysema wheeze. He was blinded, coughing and bleeding, and that's when I noticed the wallet sticking out of his slacks.

Hoping he was a solid blackjack player, I snatched the little piece of leather and ran toward the door, not stopping to help Doreen, telling myself I wasn't a complete shit human because all that noise had to prompt a 911 call from somebody.

The dead sprint down the stairs, out of the apartment and up the hill towards Temple, left me short of breath and stumbling. At some point, the adrenaline gave out and I remembered that I'd forgotten my shoes. The cement bit hard into my feet, causing me to skid to a stop against the wall of the county courthouse.

I was shirtless, barefoot, red-faced, wearing only jeans. I turned to my right and found an old black man, clearly homeless, his face as haggard and slack as mine, dressed in about the same outfit. He was lying next to an orange tent, the kind that dotted every freeway underpass.

I tried to remind myself that we were different. That I had Doreen's watches. And Geoff's wallet. And a meeting. All he had were four or five teeth and a residence that would get knocked down by a strong wind.

As I caught my breath, I noticed a small group of twenty-somethings laughing their way up the hill, a cluster of couples probably headed home from the Little Tokyo bar scene. They got near us—too close for their comfort—and one of the men tugged his girlfriend's arm as he eyed us suspiciously.

I looked down at the soles of my feet, at the little cuts opening from my shoeless sidewalk sprint. I looked down at the homeless man's, found the same gashes scabbed over.

The sight was enough to get me moving again in spite of the bloody soles. I half-jogged toward the bus stop a block away, rounding the corner towards 1st Street just in time to catch the taillights of the 10 bus as it headed west. An El Niño-sponsored gust kicked away the exhaust cloud, giving me a momentary reprieve before the blast sent my arms racing toward my shoulders.

It does actually get cold in L.A. sometimes. Forty degrees with no shirt was enough to chill the film of sweat I'd picked up running away from Doreen's place. There wouldn't be another bus for a while, and there was no way I could walk to anywhere I had the option to sleep that night—especially without shoes. Geoff's wallet felt heavy in my pocket, but any cab driver worth his salt would call the cops if he picked up a half-naked fare trying to pay with crisp hundreds.

I turned back toward the hobo, and we shuddered in tandem as another gust shot between buildings and over us. He stepped halfway into his putrid citrus-toned tent, gave me a once-over, nodded, and held the flap of cloth out over his head, opening the door.

He didn't say a word as I stepped inside, and I didn't bother to thank him for the shelter. I fell into a far corner, exhausted, but happy to be out of the desert wind and off my feet. I pulled my knees to my chest and felt the haul from Doreen's apartment shuffle in each pocket, worried that my rescuer would catch a glint of the watches or see the lip of Geoff's wallet.

I looked across the tent, caught him staring. Maybe he was just confused by the idea of having company. Maybe he was sizing me up the way I'd sized up everyone else.

Didn't matter. I wasn't sleeping that night. I knew all too well how easy it was to help someone up with one hand and run their pockets with the other.

Doreen's watches. Geoff's wallet. Vanessa's ring. I'd lined them all up on Jay's coffee table, thinking about what they added up to and where they'd come from.

Two assaults. All kinds of sex that was essentially for profit. A few minutes too many spent running away from people. One night too many spent on the street.

All that for a thirty-day stay of execution. That's what the pilfered items added up to. Another security deposit. Another month's rent.

Jay didn't ask questions when I showed up on his doorstep the morning after Doreen's, looking like hammered shit and feeling worse. The last time he'd let me in his apartment I'd robbed him. But the last time I'd been there I'd probably been the cocksure asshole he had every reason to mistrust, not the pathetic filth-covered thing in front of him.

The girl who hated me was out of town, so Jay decided to let me crash until my meeting with Linda. He didn't even bring up the possibility of me stealing from him again. He probably knew he didn't have to.

My eyes wandered from my haul to the backpack leaning against the couch. I unzipped it and pulled out my laptop and the sliver of my comic book collection I'd managed to save during Vanessa's break-in.

They were the only two things I actually owned. Two things I'd brought here from New Jersey in the hopes of getting a meeting with a person like Linda.

I swept the watches and the wallet and the ring aside and placed the laptop in the center of the table, powering up the thing I used to lovingly refer to as a high-tech typewriter.

The laptop glowed to life, and I started opening up old files. Half-written scripts, treatments, episode summaries, random plot outlines that I barely remembered writing to begin with, probably because I could barely remember the last time I wrote.

Before he granted me the meeting, Jay had warned me about the difference between trying to be something and failing to be something.

In three days I'd get one more chance to try. I started typing.

I wiped a finger across my forehead, trying to stop the mix of nerves and hairspray from melting into my eyes, struggling to get comfortable in the charcoal suit I'd borrowed from Jay. He had bigger shoulders than me, and the blazer kept moving around on its own accord, making it obvious to anyone paying enough attention that I was wearing a costume.

The crowd at Perch, the rooftop bar where I was supposed to take my meeting, was a haven for successful singles. Any of the countless suits and skirts traipsing between the lounge chair clusters and cocktail stations could have been lawyers, prosecutors, reporters, City Hall types or—god forbid—cops. I assumed Linda Reyes, Jay's studio hookup, was somewhere in that mix, maybe giving me the once-over, deciding if I was worth her time.

I'd spent the past three days trying to make sure I was. Reviewing old pitches, character outlines and half-written opening scenes. Taking notes on episodes of the shows Linda ran. Scribbling some spec script options in case she asked for them.

That night at Doreen's was too much. Stealing was one thing, fending off domestic abusers with hairspray and running face-first into my Ghost of Vagrant Future was another entirely. I didn't come to L.A. to hurt anyone, and I'd committed felony assault twice in the span of a week. Maybe I'd gotten Doreen hurt in the process. If I wanted to fuck and fight all day, I could have stayed in Jersey.

My eyes scanned the room on instinct, trying to use the same skill-set I employed to target women to pick out Linda. But I kept getting stuck on potential marks. The threesome of blondes who looked too old to be happy to be single. The brunette who kept laughing too loud at her male coworker's jokes, as if she could guffaw her way past his wedding ring. The Latina girl to my left who kept checking her phone and surveying the roof, either pretending she was waiting for someone or just now realizing whoever was supposed to arrive had stood her up.

I lingered on the last one. Dark hair, plum lipstick, gold blouse and a knee-length black skirt. Lawyer uniform. No ring in sight. We locked eyes for a minute and I immediately turned away. She looked familiar, but I had a type, a profile, and maybe in a way they all looked the same. I was already coming up with a fake name, a first line.

"Are you Lonnie?"

The question came from the other direction. I turned around to find a woman standing there with one hand on her hips, the other using the bar top as a crutch, leering impatiently.

"Um, yeah?" I said as I took stock of the woman's slightly round figure, which wasn't helped by her choice of outfit: A long-sleeve gray pullover that hid whatever cleavage she might have had, but promoted the slight bulge in her midsection. The black skirt and black stockings might have helped a few pounds ago, but not now. The glasses didn't do her any favors either.

"Linda Reyes," she said, extending a hand for a shake. It didn't seem like a suggestion.

I took her hand and silently cursed myself, hoping I could shut off the part of my brain that appraised women like cattle.

"You're late and I don't have a lot of time," she said, sitting down.

"Late? I've been here waiting for you."

"You're on a job interview. It's your job to find me," she said. "We'll worry about that later. Anyway, what are you drinking?"

A bartender appeared before I could answer, and she ordered up two more of my overpriced beers.

"So, Lonnie…what made you want to get back in the game?" she asked.

"Back in?"

"You haven't had a writing credit in over three years. You don't even hold a Writer's Guild card. So what have you been doing all this time?" she asked.

Nothing much…stealing things from the women I sleep with, occasionally reselling their prescription drugs to people somehow lower on the scumbag totem pole than me.

"Surviving mostly," I said out loud, technically not lying. "It's just been tough to find work."

She let her glasses slip off her nose a bit, shot me an "I know that's bullshit" look, and took a long swallow from her freshly delivered drink.

"Well then, you're lucky I owe Jay a favor," she said. "Have you ever been a writer's assistant before?"

"Assistant?" I asked.

She shook her head and took another long sip.

"What exactly did Jay tell you this was?"

"He said it was a meeting. That you'd seen some of my stuff."

"Those student shorts?" she asked, her face twisting into a smirk that was needlessly cruel. "Yeah, he showed me enough to show me you're competent, and with time, maybe we'll get to a point where you can pitch me some ideas, but that's not how it starts."

Now it was my turn to take a long swallow.

"Lonnie," she said, leaning closer. "You haven't worked in years. For all intents and purposes, you're starting over. If you work under me, read some scripts, sit in on some writer's meetings, maybe we'll get somewhere. But don't delude yourself. This is your chance to get back in, but it's just a chance, not a promise. This is rung-one stuff."

Rung-one stuff. Nobody work. Thankless work. The kind Jay knew had driven me to operate the way I did all those years ago.

Linda downed the rest of her drink and pulled out a debit card in the same motion. She seemed like the kind of person who needed to do several things at once.

"So?" she asked.

"I'll be able to pitch eventually?"

"Eventually."

"How long is eventually?" I asked.

She let out an audible sigh.

"Listen, kid. You're getting a chance. And given your track record, maybe not one you deserve. I don't have time for an ego, and I'm certainly not begging you to work for me when I could walk down the street and find four people willing to beg me in kind," she said. "Now I'm going to ask you once if you want this job, and you're going to say yes—because the way I see it, you have to."

I thought about my other options, and realized none of them involved a career path. I saw the Latina woman across the bar, still playing with her phone, and thought about the dozens of ways I could get her into bed that night and the hundreds of things that could go wrong after.

"Yeah," I said before Linda could even ask the question. "I'm in."

That same cruel smirk spread across her face again, then it softened into something less threatening. She put a hand on my shoulder.

"Good call, Lonnie," she said. "Jay did send me some of your pitches. A few of them had promise. Stick with me, and maybe we can eventually do something with one or two. But you gotta earn it. Understand?"

That hand traveled up my shoulder to the back of my neck, catching a strand of my hair. She tugged on it, like it was a leash.

"Um, Ms. Reyes?" I asked.

"Oh good, you picked up on that already. It's best we stay formal in public."

"I'm not sure what you're thinking here," I said, even though I absolutely did.

"Honey, I've got a pile of resumes on my desk from film school students. You think Jay got my attention based on your accomplishments?" she asked. "He told me about your...proclivities. That's why I got us a hotel room down the street. This way you can earn your keep and I can keep my wallet."

I thought about the look on Doreen's face when she was on top, and realized Linda was wearing the exact same expression. Satisfaction, maybe even victory. I wanted to shout, scream, curse at this woman for thinking I'd whore myself out for the chance to fetch her coffee.

But I'd spent years whoring myself out for less. At least this might end with a pension.

Linda's hand moved to my face, rubbing my cheek the way you might pet something, and I clasped it and gave it a little peck, a silent acknowledgment of my new place on the ladder.

That's the problem with living life on the prowl. Sooner or later, every predator becomes something else's prey.

THUGLIT

Tulare
by Blair Kroeber

They could have been on the moon, the land was so barren. The valley floor, stretching every way into darkness, so thirsty. After three years of drought, the crops around them—almond trees mostly, pistachio groves beyond those—thrived in defiance of the parched conditions.

The boy, Colby, seized the brim of his ball cap and slid it around backwards. He was hunched on a knee beside Trav at the base of the huge rotary drill. In his front teeth he clenched the rubber grip of a pocket flashlight, its beam bobbling across the technical docs perched on his knee. The kid had done his homework, sleuthing out schematics for the drill online somewhere. Good—Trav had certainly paid him enough to earn the extra effort.

"You want me to hold the light for you?" Trav's voice, a rasp in the shadows.

Colby jittered his head side-to-side, his concentration fixed on the pages before him. He lifted his face, leveling the flashlight beam into the drill's exposed wirework. "These here, I think they're the fuel intake valves," he said, plucking the flashlight from his lips and pointing with it.

"Yeah?"

"I think."

"Sounds like a good place to start," Trav said. "Rip them out."

The boy replaced the flashlight in his mouth, drew out a pair of pliers. Metal clinked metal as he fiddled with the valve nozzles. Trav turned, scanned their surroundings. Only those half-bare almond trees, neat rows of them, reaching their fingers into the blackness. Beyond that, far across the flatness of the valley, the shadowed ridges of the Sierra foothills regressed into darkness.

Warm wind breathed around them. The kid's pliers clinked and clanked. Trav footed a slow circle. He was still a few years shy of forty, but he moved with the gait of an older man. His eyes, scanning again. The two of them were plenty alone. Another thirty minutes, minimum, before he could expect the security patrol to come cycling around. An hour at least til he'd hear screen doors push open, see the early risers come steering down the nearby blacktop. Those ranchers, work hands, laborers, they'd be well in advance of sunrise, but that was the problem with farmers—they kept farmers' hours.

The almond trees, like the massive drill, belonged to Galinger Farmworks, one of the two remaining family-owned agribusinesses of any real size in this pocket of the Central Valley. Trav had known the Galingers his whole life. He'd attended grade school and then high school with their eldest, Pete. As a boy, Trav had even visited their home a couple times, though all he could recall now was the mother's collection of ostrich eggs, which she kept under glass in a lighted display case, and the father's hunting trophies, the antlered elk and fanged cougar heads that lined the walls. They were fancy folks, the Galingers. But weird. Cruel somehow.

Six, seven years back, Pete had inherited control of their growing enterprise. The drill, a recent addition, purchased from a bankrupt fracking outfit in Wyoming, had been his idea, an effort to counter the effects of the drought. With it, he could bore deeper into the underground aquifers—thousands of feet down, further than his father or grandfather had ever dreamed.

This monstrosity of a machine? Trav had been looking forward to dismantling it.

He rounded back to Colby. "You got this or what?" Anxiety seeped into his tone. His nerves were jangling like school bells.

"Jesus Christ," the kid breathed, "gimme a second. It's not like changing a light bulb." He set the pliers on his knee, cracked the knuckles of one hand. "You know how much these things cost?"

"Deep six-digits, at least."

"Exactly. They're pricey. We're talking quality engineering, meaning they don't break easily. You feel me?"

Trav didn't like the kid's mouth, but he let him alone. If Colby couldn't hobble the drill, no one in Trav's orbit could swing the task. The boy worked as a grease monkey in town, but he had a brain for bigger things. He'd even enrolled himself in a couple electrical engineering classes at the UC extension some years back. Had he been born a hundred-seventy miles to the south, in Los Angeles, he would have been programming defense systems on fighter jets at Raytheon or Northrop Grumman by now. Instead, he'd been born here in the valley to half-wit parents, which had consigned him to repairing more earthbound vehicles usually stickered with brand-names like John Deere or Massey Ferguson.

Trav put his back to the machine and appraised the night once more. From the west, a sound came creeping on the wind. His back ramrodded, his head jerked up. A pair of headlights were bouncing down the rutted auto track that bisected the almond grove.

Security.

Two nights surveilling the place, and Trav had never seen them approach their direction, or at that time.

"Shit." He slapped the kid. "Guards are coming. Let's tuck out."

Colby didn't bicker. He bundled his pouch of tools under his arm, grabbed his paperwork. The wheels of the 4x4, audibly crunching over hardpack, trundled in toward the rig as they ducked away through the tanks and pipes of the drill apparatus, clambering over a hillock of dry earth and dropping out of sight. Headlights fanned across the mound where they hid. Trav, splayed on his back, tried to flatten himself into the dust, his bad hip pulsing out pain. Beside him, Colby lay on his stomach, fighting to control the gasp of his breath. They swapped a look as the vehicle slowed.

"If they stop, it means we're made," Trav said in a hush. "Just bolt."

"How would they have made us? I thought you knocked out the surveillance cams two nights ago."

"I did, which means they didn't. So sit tight and keep cool, alright?"

Trav went very still, straining to listen. The engine-rumble was receding. The guards hadn't spotted a thing. They were simply passing through, patrolling by rote.

Trav waited til the sound vanished, then he beckoned the kid. "All good."

They clambered afoot, sweeping dust and pebbles from their clothes. Only then did Trav take in the full sight of the hillock they'd used for cover. It was the lip of some depression, shallow but almost crater-like, wide enough to encompass the drill base and much of the almond grove in its bowl.

"Christ," Trav said.

Colby followed his gaze. "What is it?"

Trav pointed. "See this basin? They've leeched too much moisture from the water table. Ground-level's sinking." He lifted his eyes to the drill. "C'mon, let's get this done."

They moved back to the drill housing. Colby knelt to the open console and went back to work. Soon he was jabbing a finger at something within. "Well, looky here."

"What do you got?"

The kid pointed to some dark mass amidst the tangle of wires. "Circuit board. I think it's for the guidance system." He must have seen Trav react to those words, *guidance system*, because he broke into a grin. "I know, right? Telling you, these things are souped to heaven, man. But that's where you hit 'em. Not on the hardware..." He gestured to the broken fuel valve nozzles hanging in his pocket, "...but on the software. The sensitive parts."

"Do it then. Gut it."

Still grinning, the boy reached in, both hands rummaging past wiring to clench, pull.

Far away to the east, a warbling wail rose on the air, echoing across the valley.

"Fire siren," Trav said. "There's a burn somewhere."

Colby ignored the sound, tugging at the circuit board within the drill rig. The siren sound lingered for long seconds, until a chorus of wild yips peaked over it. Coyotes, roused by the noise, shouting their reply. And then nearer—the muffled bark of a dog trapped indoors somewhere, roaring at the coyotes. Trav had seen the ranch foreman driving the property by day, often with his German Shepherd skittering in the truck bed. Could be they resided someplace close by. A trailer, maybe? Somewhere in the grove? Farm workers did that sort of thing. If the guy woke up, if he decided to loose his dog outside to pee or chase the coyotes, they'd be screwed.

The din rising around them, Trav peered down at Colby. "We need to roll."

Colby, straining, pulling. "Gimme one more second."

Trav footed in a circle, trying to track the sound of the foreman's dog. A warm breeze rustled through the almond trees. Far off, the coyotes shrieked. Trav's stomach had gone fluttery. His chest was slamming.

Colby broke loose the circuit board, wrenched it from the drill housing. "Voila."

Trav took the board and pulled the kid to his feet. "Atta' boy. Now c'mon, quick."

They had brought fireworks with them, the cheapest form of detonative they could put their hands on. Trav had planned to drop a couple of the Roman candles into the rig to burn out the wiring, just for the merriment of it all. No time now.

They strode into blackness, crunching across the earth toward the distant corner of the grove where Trav had parked his pickup. Somewhere a door whined open, and the dog roared louder, loose now. Tags jangling, its baying rose and turned frantic.

It had forgotten the coyotes, scenting them instead.

It was sprinting their way.

"Dog's coming," Trav said, his voice barely controlled. "Let's kick it up."

They broke into a jog as the frenzied howls of the German Shepherd echoed through the almond trees. They sprinted the last distance, Trav falling behind, gripping at his bum hip as he ran all stiff-legged. Colby ducked through the fence, held the barbed-wire for Trav, and they beelined for the truck.

They reached the cab, and Trav fumbled for his keys. In the rearview, the massive dog came ripping out of the grove, all hackles, ears perked, teeth shining. It cut the distance toward the truck as Trav roared the engine alive. Last he saw in the mirror was the snarling canine turning red with the glow of his taillights as he hit the accelerator and tore across the dirt.

Three nights before, Lacey had phoned him, asking for a meet-up at the derelict Safeway store out on Schulz Road, south of the 99.

The call piqued his interest.

Lacey never phoned him.

She never asked for a meet-up.

Trav arrived early to suss out the place, squirming his way through the pinewood panel boards they'd nailed over the broken glass of the entry, grunting when he tweaked his hip. Inside, he rubbed out the pain and waited for his eyes to adjust to the clammy darkness. No security lights in there. Nothing. The store had shuttered several years ago, during the recession that preceded the drought. Trav couldn't figure why the property owners would allow the place to lay deserted like this. Apparently they had bigger problems, like everyone else right now.

Trav shuffled ahead into the dusty blackness, toeing at empty beer cans, condom wrappers. Probing that interior was like spelunking through the carcass of some vast primordial beast. He'd never had occasion to consider the sheer square footage of your average grocery store, but he noticed it now, wandering long aisles of empty shelving, much of it half-dismantled. Toward the back, in the one-time bakery section, he found two methheads nodding on a ratty chaise cushion and rousted them out of the place.

Soon headlights came glowing through the boarded-up entry at front, throwing slats of light up the aisles. A car door opened, clunked shut. The headlights stayed on as Lacey came easing, cat-like, between the pine panels. Pulling her leg through behind her, she tossed her head and those dark curls unraveled across her shoulders. She took in the wreckage of the building interior and then locked onto Trav, bouncing on her feet, all different colors of nervous. Dust worked though the headlight-glow between them.

"You alone?" Trav said.

"Yeah. Brett doesn't know anything about this." Brett—her husband. Managed the fertilizer plant in town. "He never cared much about the particulars of the family business, long as my share of the profits made its way into our checking account."

"That's what we're meeting about, then?" Trav said. "Your farming outfit?"

Lacey's family, the Brancusos, ran Sand Hollow Ranch, the vast plot of farmland that abutted Galinger Farmworks. Going back generations, longer than Trav or Lacey or Pete had been alive, folks in the valley had joked about the rivalry between the two families. The jokes were not particularly funny, and mostly true.

Lacey nodded and sifted her foot through the trash on the floor, carving lines in the dust. "We're in rough shape, Trav. I'm worried about Daddy's heart, his blood pressure. We had to furlough half our people last month."

"How come?"

"Heinz pulled their contract because we fallowed a quarter of the fields last year. Said we were trying to sabotage our own output to wiggle out of the arrangement. You believe that? They're punishing us for letting our fields lie fallow."

She snuffled at the idiocy of it, and her eyes explored the shadows. There was uncertainty and despair in her gaze. Trav hated seeing it there. For nearly two-thirds of his life, Lacey had occupied real estate in his heart. Like a squatter who takes up residence and refuses to leave.

They'd gone together one autumn, years ago, early in high school. It was a different time in the valley then—the air had been cool and moist that fall. There was beauty in the dying of the trees, the turning of the seasons. The first time they made love, it was in the park near her parents' house. After it was done, they had lain naked on the dewy grass. Trav never stopped associating that fecund smell of wet earth with Lacey and their time together. Even now, the mere sight of her, just the fact of her presence there in such proximity to his own, it left him feeling filleted open. Vulnerable. Frightened.

"But honestly, Trav," she said, "this move from Heinz, that's not even the biggest problem we got. What's really

162

fucking us is this drill the Galingers bought. You heard about this?"

"I'm aware of it, yeah," Trav said. It was true. He made a habit of following developments in the region, ever since honing his reputation as a go-to guy.

He had been a sheriff's deputy once. Til the night he answered an armed robbery call. Liquor store on Route 137. A gangbanger—Salvadoran kid, MS-13—had just capped the Sikh guy behind the register. As Trav stepped from the patrol car, the boy opened fire on him, too. A 9mm round caught Trav in the hip before he could put the kid down. Thirteen days in the hospital, four surgeries. Lacey had sent flowers, but never managed to visit in person.

Trav could have taken a desk job with the department, but the county's law enforcement budget, gutted by recession-driven cutbacks, could only accommodate able-bodied officers. The sheriff suggested they get the doctors to sign off on permanent disability. Trav was out of the workforce by his thirty-fourth birthday.

But the heart wants what the heart wants, right?

And his wanted back in the action.

He started picking up tasks. This-and-that sort of things. He worked the door, off the books, at the Dust Devil Saloon; then he began collecting for their off-hour poker games. If one of the regular guys needed a favor, Trav would wade in, knuckle-up the relevant parties. A busted hip, after all, didn't affect his ability to throw a fist.

Got to the point where he was open to most opportunities, so long as they kept him on that brighter side of the right-and-wrong line.

Standing before Lacey now, massaging his old injury, all giddy with that filleted-open feeling, he asked about the Galingers' drill.

"It's a beast," she said. "Damn thing can penetrate up to two thousand feet underground. Like the rest of us, Pete's desperate to get at the groundwater. Right before the drought started, he switched their tomato and onion fields over to nut trees. Pistachios, chestnuts, particularly the almonds—"

"They command higher prices," Trav said.

Lacey nodded. "For export, especially. The Chinese love that stuff. We're talking over a billion people, most of them only now developing a taste for almonds. The one problem? All those nuts, they require year-round water. A shit-ton of it." She gestured around her. "But we've got dust bowl conditions, and now the feds have begun rationing reserves from the Sac River Basin."

Trav shifted onto his good hip and let off a low whistle. "What a fix..."

"And you know Pete Galinger—he's not the fuck-around sort. He sued the federal agencies. Then sued them again. When they countersued, he met their suit with another of his own. But these lawsuits, they're slow-moving endeavors. Pete, like the rest of us, needs water now."

"Hence the drill, " Trav said, giving a head-shake.

Lacey began trembling, and her voice cracked. "That's the thing, though, Trav—he's leeching the aquifers dry. Draining out all the deposits." Somewhere in the darkness, a bird exploded out of the rafters, the flapping sound echoing around them. Lacey ignored it. She rubbed at the back of her neck, her anxiety climbing. "And you know where my family's plot sits in relation to theirs. Given the depth of the Galingers' well, they're slurping up all the groundwater for acres in every direction. There won't be anything left after this. It's fucking robbery."

Stooped there in the darkness, Trav was coming to see the shape of the thing, grasping now why Lacey had reached out to him.

"Somebody has got to do something about that drill," she said, her voice quivering. "What do you say, Trav? Can you help me out?"

But surely she already knew he would.

LAST WRITES

The morning after their visit to the Galinger property, Trav started getting antsy. Better put, his nerves from the previous night simply refused to abate. Had the foreman come outside for his dog and spotted them? Anyone else made his truck as they hightailed out of there? He knew with certainty that the damage to the drill had been discovered—he'd seen a blurb in the Times-Delta crime blotter—but had they traced it to him and the boy?

He had one good option: to feel out his law-enforcement people.

If they suspected him, he would catch the signs.

So by mid-afternoon, he had settled himself at the counter of Dinah's, the preferred 10-46 location for the on-duty patrol officers. He was nursing his third cup of coffee by the time Deputy Leary—Theresa, to a former fellow officer—came pushing through the door of the diner. He waited for her to settle into a booth and place her order before he hobbled over, exaggerating his limp, and pretended to notice her there. They rapped for a minute or two—small talk, drought conditions, her kids, the department's shitty new 401(k)—before Trav circled around to the Galingers' drill. Any movement on the investigation?

He played it envious. "Days like this one," he said, "weird crimes rearing up, I truly do miss the job."

"Can't say I blame you. This one's a doozy."

"How do you mean?"

Theresa lifted her coffee cup to her lips and snickered as she did, so that steam huffed out. She took a slow sip, likely considering how much she could divulge, but Trav was a friend. She smirked at him over her mug. "Check it out, we get a call this morning, right? Insurance guy, claims assessor. Wants to know if we like anyone for the deed. Sounds like they suspect an inside thing. Pete installed the drill three months ago, but just took out the policy week before last."

"The drill was insured, huh?"

"Sure was," Theresa said. "Pete Galinger, clever cat, got himself a hefty policy. And wouldn't you know it? Industrial sabotage is covered."

Trav supplied the reaction she wanted, reeling on his feet. "Damn..." He mugged surprise. Truth was, he felt it too.

Theresa rocked in her seat, all cynical, derisive. The chapped leather of the booth bench squeaked. "Betcha this insurance guy is right, too."

"That Pete busted his own drill, you mean?"

She nodded. "Couple of the older fellas with the department, guys with long memories, say Pete's father tried the same stunt with a crop-duster back in the seventies. Pulled it off, too. They could never make the charges stick." She shrugged, grimly amused. "Same here, I bet. The family money will insulate him. We'll never peg this thing on Pete."

Trav genuinely balked, then scrambled to downplay the reaction. But as he headed for the door, the world seemed to tilt and whirl around him. Sound died away. Everything ebbed to a slow-mo crawl as his mind ticked through it.

An insurance policy, a potential payout.

And if Pete was working an angle, it meant Lacey was tied in.

Goddamnit, they had used him.

So smoothly, too. So easily.

Outside, the sunlight sapped him. The thought of Lacey's role, it made him shiver in the listless heat. He suddenly felt cold and used up and heartsick. Then quickly the despair bloomed into something more useful—anger. They had exploited him for their own gain. They had leveraged his affection. Never again.

He had to get back on the bright side of the line.

The winter sun, rust-colored, was sliding to the earth as he drove out to the far verge of town. Lacey's home was a raised ranch-style place perched at the northwestern corner of her family's acreage. Trav took up a post in the turnabout down the road, watching the house in his mirrors. He had swapped out his pickup for the Olds beater his pops had left behind after kicking off. Lacey wouldn't know the car. Still, feeling cautious, Trav had smeared mud over the plates, front and back.

All that night, the next morning—nothing.

But the following evening—pay dirt.

Apparently Lacey's hubs had picked up a swing-shift, because she was alone when Pete arrived after sundown, carrying a bottle of something in a brown bag. They were toasting, celebrating. Lacey met Pete at the front door, her lips an over-painted pink, and pressed her mouth against his. The kitchen light winked out as they moved upstairs. Trav thought he could hear the bed pitching and groaning beneath them.

Made no sense. Going back four generations, their families had been set against each other. If they were going to step out on their spouses, why do it with one another?

Then again, the heart wants what the heart wants, doesn't it?

Apparently Lacey and Pete, they were living some Romeo and Juliet fantasy—rival families, forbidden romance…all that tired-out horseshit.

And hadn't the arrangement checked other boxes too? The drill was out of operation. Lacey had protected her family's future. Hell, maybe that was why she'd initiated the fling in the first place, to manipulate Pete to her purpose. No doubt once she made the ask, Pete sensed opportunity. A chance to make some scratch off the arrangement.

Friends with benefits, indeed.

But no way could Trav let this scam of theirs roll ahead.

He hunched in the driver's seat, gripping the wheel so hard, the blood drained out of his hands. Outside, the air reeked of manure. The smell of it leaking into the vehicle.

What did he know? And how could he use that knowledge to swamp this thing?

Here, for one: the sheriff deputies, his old cohorts, already held an inkling of suspicion toward Pete. Trav could firm up those suspicions—he still had the stolen drill parts in his keeping. Maybe he ought to plant them on the Galingers' land? Use Colby, a voice the sheriff's dispatch wouldn't recognize, to lob a tip to Theresa or some other curious someone at the station?

Trav's guts clenched. His stomach, burning. This plan of his, it didn't hang together, not yet. The big wrinkle: even if he made Pete for busting his own drill, Lacey could still get off, potentially, so long as Pete decided not to roll over on her. Now there was a twist—Pete's drill would be out of action, her family's aquifers protected. She'd skate clean, her goals realized.

Jesus.

Unless he squirreled the evidence on her property. A move like that put her in a genuine pickle, didn't it? Either she took the rap for both of them, or she tattled on Pete, revealing their affair, blowing up her marriage and her family's reputation.

Yeah, Trav liked the idea.

Very least, he would get to watch her squirm.

This time of year, so long after full dark, the valley floor should have been cottoned with fog. Instead, all was desiccation. A meek wind whispering out of the eastern foothills, but only now and again, as if Mother Nature couldn't decide whether she wanted to shout.

Trav had driven a rounder back to his place for the circuit board, the fuel nozzles. Returning to Lacey's, creeping across the land around her house, he could tell the pair of them had finished their action upstairs and come back down to the kitchen. A murmur of voices filtered from the glowing windows, and shapes loomed past the curtains now and again.

Fumbling in darkness, Trav located the access lid for the septic tank, pried it open. Seemed a good spot for the disposal of evidence. But maybe too good. What if the authorities got lazy and didn't go dredging into the soup of piss and muck down here? He clunked the lid back into place and doubled back to the carport instead, burying the drill parts in a barrel of greasy mechanic's tools. Hard to miss there, so long as someone made even a half-assed effort to search the grounds.

Trav returned to the Olds and crouched behind the wheel, rubbing at the knotty joint of his thigh, gaming it all. A new concern. What if Lacey didn't fold on Pete? What if she let him walk free and clear? Trav couldn't tolerate the notion. There had to be some kind of recompense for the rich prick. But maybe Trav could handle that part himself.

He held his watch til Pete, wasted, came shambling out the door and dropped into the driver's seat of his fancy Carrera. The car ripped down the empty blacktop of the road, weaving back and forth across the lane. Trav woke the Olds, dropped it into gear, and followed, driving without headlights. He needed to catch Pete isolated, unaware.

Almost immediately the drunk bastard gave him the chance. A couple miles out from the Farmworks property, the Carrera went bumping onto the dusty shoulder of the road. Trav crept his vehicle onto the hardpack some ways back, watching. Pete clambered out of the Porsche and shambled over to one of his own irrigation ditches to drain his bladder.

Trav climbed from the Olds, moved noiselessly. Pete, teetering on his feet, urine slapping into the dust, didn't even notice the dark figure advancing on him. Not til Trav sunk a blow into the softness of his lower back, striking at the kidney.

The wind was calling louder now—it had raised its voice finally, growling from the east to hiss about them. Trav swung Pete around and landed another punch. The guy let off a low grunt and went into the ditch, hitting the opposite embankment. Anger simmered through Trav as he followed him down and buried his fist in the ruddy flesh of Pete's face.

He seized a fistful a wispy hair and pulled the man's head toward his own. "You or Lacey get popped and implicate me in this thing of yours, no amount of money can ever protect you, got it? I'll come creeping around. Maybe I'll see if Lacey's husband wants to pitch in, too." Pete's eyes were lolling. He couldn't pull focus. But Trav could tell he recognized the voice.

One blow, another...

Pete went out, his chin bobbing against his chest. Pecker still dangling loose from his zipper. Trav felt all hot relief, a pot seeping out steam. He forced himself to cut it off before he did any more damage.

Best to conserve energy, too. He had to stay sharp til morning, when he would go around to collect Colby, make their calls and finish this business. The pain that Lacey had given him, he'd stuff it down deep and crawl his way back across the line.

Somewhere an owl screamed, falling on its prey. Dead branches clicked in the breeze. Trav dragged Pete down into a low hollow, clear of any sight-lines from above, then he slumped against the dusty lip of the ditch, breathing hard, rubbing his aching fingers and knuckles.

LAST WRITES

Fury kept pulsing through him, hot like that valley wind. He threw another glance down to Pete. He could very well kill the guy right there, but the aqueduct, at its bottom, held only a thin trickle of moisture. There wasn't even enough water for drowning.

THUGLIT

Slant Six
by S.A. Cosby

"That for sale?" the customer asked.

I walked from under the truck that was suspended on the hydraulic rack and sat my socket wrench down on the red three-level toolbox. I pulled a rag out of my pocket and wiped my paws. The rag didn't clean my hands, just moved the dirt to more acceptable locations. He was pointing at the Plymouth Duster sitting kitty-cornered in the far end of my garage. It was usually covered by a heavy canvas tarp, but I had taken it out for a ride this morning and hadn't put the cover on it yet. It was candy-apple red with chrome mag rims and black leather seats. A black racing stripe zipped down its side before narrowing to a point as it reached the front fender wall. The stick shift was an 8-ball and the gas pedal was a metal foot. I moved closer to the customer who had moved closer to the Duster.

"No, it's not for sale," I said.

The customer frowned. Then he took a step closer to the car. "What's she got in her?" he asked.

"225 slant-six bored out. It come from the factory with four on the floor but my daddy popped that out and dropped a five-speed in her and then bored cylinders out to accommodate the overdrive gear," I said. The customer whistled.

"What will she do in the flat?" he asked. I shrugged.

"Haven't timed it in awhile. But she will do seventy in third," I said.

The customer grunted. "Your daddy must have been one hell of a gearhead," he said.

"He was a hell of a lot of things," I said.

I don't think the customer heard me.

The last time I'd ridden in that car with my daddy was the summer I turned thirteen. The Chicago Bears were just laying the foundations for what would become the greatest defense in football history. Reagan was doddering through his second term after giving Mondale the most epic ass-kicking in political history. I had been sitting on the cinderblock steps of the single-wide trailer I shared with my mom, playing with some second-rate action figures Daddy had given me for my last birthday.

I heard the Duster before I saw it. It sounded like the thunder from one of those storms that formed out of nothing and dropped a foot of rain on you before you could say Noah's Ark. I raised my head and shielded my eyes from the sun. I saw it then. The car was careening down the long dusty lane that served as our driveway. It left a cloud of dust and grit in its wake.

Our trailer sat a good mile and a half off the main highway. My daddy was covering that distance as fast as a bolt of lightning. He came up into our yard and slammed on the brakes while twisting the steering wheel around one and half times. The Duster did one complete revolution. The ground was horribly dry, so the cloud of dust that enveloped the car appeared otherworldly.

Daddy parked the car and popped the emergency brake. He emerged from the dust cloud like the superhero I had convinced myself he was. Tall and brown like a caramel-dipped Goliath. He was wearing a black short-sleeved button-up shirt that was open at the throat, exposing his massive neck. Under the shirt he was wearing a ribbed tank top tee-shirt that has since been christened a wifebeater.

"You ready Bug?" he said. His voice boomed across the yard, startling the cardinals in the magnolia tree next to our trailer. Before I could answer, my mother came to the door. I heard the hinges creak as she opened it.

"Anthony, you bring some money, or is all of it in that damn car?" my mother asked.

"Jean, I just wanna spend some time with my boy before...I just wanna spend some time with Bug."

"His name is Beauregard," she said. I turned my head and saw her standing there puffing away on a cigarette. I could feel it pass between them. The anger, the frustration, and something else I was too young to appreciate. My mother had her long silky hair up in a bun. When she let it down, it would fall to her hips. A lot of people would say they had Native American blood, but couldn't tell a Cree from an Apache. My grandma was full-blooded Pamunkey and my mother had inherited her sharp cheekbones and her midnight waterfall of hair.

"I know that, Jean. But he likes Bug just like I like Ant," Daddy said.

"Anthony, we have a half a loaf of bread and some scrapple in the fridge. I don't get paid from the plant until next week. I'm glad you wanna spend time with Beauregard but we can't eat your good intentions," she said.

"Look, Jean—I just wanna take the boy for a ride. When I come back we can talk. I'll even go to the Safeway and get some neckbones and broth and make us a soup. But right now I need to be with Bu...Beauregard," my daddy said. I saw the shimmer of possibilities wash across my mama's face. If Daddy was talking about making soup, he might be talking about spending the night. My parents were married, but my daddy had made it clear long ago he would leave his boots under different beds from time to time. I don't know why Mama just didn't divorce him. Love has many faces I guess. It can even look like hate on occasion.

"Go on then, Anthony. Just go on," she said. I heard the door slam shut.

"Well, that went about as well as I expected. You ready to go, boy?" Daddy asked.

"Yep," I said.

"Well, come on, get your ass in the car! What you waiting for, Christmas?" he said. I hopped up off the steps and jogged over to the car. I got in the passenger side and he slipped in the driver's seat. We didn't bother putting on seatbelts. My daddy drove so fast, if we did wreck, seatbelts would just be in the way when the undertakers tried to get us out.

"You ready? We gonna see what she got. I say she got enough to make a midget stand tall," Daddy said. I laughed. He laughed too. We took off spinning tires and kicking up dirt as we rocketed down the lane. We hit the road in second and my daddy cranked the steering wheel to the left and for a minute I swore we were going up on two wheels. He dropped it into third and we were flying down the double-lane blacktop road that snaked through Mathews County. Trees and houses were just blurs as we zipped down the road. He flipped on the radio and the Mighty Rev. Al Green's angelic falsetto dripped from the speakers.

"You scared, boy?" Daddy asked.

"Not if you ain't," I said. He grinned at me and I grinned back. We probably looked like a couple of lunatics. But that was alright because it was okay to be a little crazy with your daddy on a hot summer day in a car that felt like Hermes himself was pushing you along.

"I'm gonna hit in fourth and I want you to try and touch the dash," he said. I grinned even wider. This was an old game. The torque on the engine was so tight that when he hit fourth gear the g-forces would pin me and my thirteen-year-old frame to the seat. I knew instinctively that the day I could touch the dash would be the day I left boyhood behind. Daddy slammed it into fourth and the engine screamed like a demon born in the hottest pits of hell. I felt a powerful pressure on my bird chest as I stretched my hands out, vainly trying to touch the dash.

"You ain't man enough yet, boy, but dammit if you ain't getting there!" Daddy cackled.

We slid into the North Star Mart doing thirty miles per hour. Daddy pulled up to the gas pumps and hopped out with an agility that shouldn't have come so easy to a man of his size. He went inside the store. When he came out he had a brown paper bag in his hand. He pumped the gas, then got back in the car. He twisted the cap off of the bottle in the bag and damn near killed it with one gulp.

"Daddy, why is Mama always mad at you?" I asked. Daddy smiled, but it never reached his eyes. He started the car and turned up the radio. Now it was WAR kicking the speakers in the ass.

"I think you mama still mad at herself for falling for my bullshit. So she takes it out on me," he said. He dropped the car in gear and we zoomed out of the parking lot. We passed Mr. Mcready on his ancient rust-covered tractor and took a hard right onto Ridge Road. Majestic pine trees lined the road and made strange shadows out of the sunshine.

"Bug, I want you know that no matter what, you my son and I love you. I love you so much. But I'm gonna be going for a little while," he said as we flew down the road. We came up on a curve that was sharp enough to slice cheese and Daddy took it at forty-five without even downshifting. He just pushed in the clutch and let momentum carry us through. I had dropped my head. My daddy had been going away for as long as I could remember.

"Now while I'm gone, you mind you Mama. It's gonna be hard for both of y'all. I ain't gonna be able to send no money. So you gonna have to be good. Don't be fighting in school unless a motherfucker really deserve it." He glanced my way and saw my head hanging down.

"But I ain't leaving today, soldier. Today we gonna ride and put Ol' Red through her paces. Then we gonna go to the Safeway and get them neckbones. Then we gonna go to the Tastee-Freeze and get some milkshakes your mama ain't gotta know nothing about," he said. He winked at me—and damned fool that I was, I smiled and winked back.

We pulled into the Safeway and I trailed behind Daddy as we entered the store. I was too big to ride in the basket, but he let me hang on the front of it like some figurehead on a Viking ship. We grabbed neckbones and potatoes and broth and carrots and peas and some biscuits in a can. As we stood in line waiting to get checked out, a man who smelled like pipe tobacco came up to us.

"Hey Ant," he said. He was thin as filament with watery sad eyes.

"Hey Deacon," Daddy said. His voice was low. The thin man stepped closer to my father.

"Red Maslin been looking for you," Deacon said.

Daddy shrugged. "Let him look," he said. Deacon's eyes seemed to become even sadder.

"Ant...he ain't buying your story. You get two years and his little brother get fifteen. It don't look good on you," Deacon said.

My father grabbed Deacon's hand. To the casual observer it was just two friends shaking. But I could see Deacon wince as my father squeezed his mustard-colored hand.

"You talk to Red again, you tell him I'm a lot of things, but a snitch ain't one of them. Blue is doing fifteen cause he got caught with that money. I just drove. You tell Red I'm gonna do my time and I'm gonna keep my mouth shut. He should do the same," he said. When he released

Deacon's hand, I could make out his handprints on Deacon's palm.

"Sure Ant. But I'd still watch my back if I was you," Deacon said. He faded into the grocery traffic like a ghost. We paid for our food and got back in the Duster.

"Who are Red and Blue, Daddy?" I asked once we had gotten back on the road.

"Two brothers who ain't nearly as bad or as smart as they think they are," he mumbled. All the fun we had been having seemed to have dried up and evaporated in the summer heat. The Duster didn't have AC, so we drove with the windows down. If you stuck your head out the window, the wind would fill your lungs like you were drowning in air. Daddy whipped the car past Old Man Cutcheon's farm and over a small bridge that covered Croaker Creek. By the time we pulled up to the Tastee-Freeze I was ready to go home and play with my action figures or read my Stephen King book.

Daddy had gone from Mr. Fantastic to Sullen Sam in the span of five minutes. The Tastee-Freeze was à la carte only. You placed your order, then you passed the clerk your money through a ragged sliding screen window. It was an anachronism that refused to acknowledge that it was obsolete.

"You want a chocolate shake or vanilla?" my daddy asked.

"Chocolate. Chocolate is my favorite," I said. Suddenly I was irritated that he didn't know the flavor of my favorite milkshake. The spell he had cast earlier had been broken. I remembered the countless days he hadn't shown up after promising to come get me. The school plays he had missed. The Christmas mornings that found him just getting home as I was waking up to open my gifts. I saw him staring at me out the corner of my eye. He was biting his lip. He started to say something, then let it go and got out of the car.

I didn't notice the IROC pull up behind us or the three men who spilled out of it. I was lost in a pity party of one. Daddy had left the car running in neutral with the emergency brake locked. I watched as he stood in front of the sliding window and paid for our shakes, a man whose face showed me what I would look like in twenty years. He turned and starting walking back to the car.

The three men intercepted him. They were white men. Rough men in jeans and black t-shirts with the sleeves rolled up to their broad shoulders. The biggest man had a shock of black hair and a red birthmark on his neck the size of a fifty-cent piece.

"What you say, Red?" Daddy said.

Red bore his eyes into my daddy's face but Daddy didn't drop his gaze. "You fucked up. You know that right? Blue doing three nickels because you couldn't keep your mouth shut," Red said. His tone was conversational but his body language promised violence.

Daddy shook his head. "Nope. Blue doing the nickels cause he couldn't sit on the money like he was supposed to. He started buying Corvettes and crack whores. Deputies ain't got shit to do but look out the window and see who driving what and who screwing who. Blue might as well have held up a sign that said *I knocked over the Cronkin Seafood Company payroll truck*. None of that lays on me."

"It do if you lying. It do if you cut a fucking deal," Red said. His voice was harsh. It was the sound a blade made scraping against bone when you skinned a deer.

Daddy looked toward the Duster. Towards me. "I ain't lying, Red. I know you don't believe me. But we ain't gotta do this in front of my son," he said.

Red pulled up his shirt so Daddy could see the butt of the gun that was stuck in his waistband. "Why not, Ant? It'll do the boy good to see what happens to snitches," Red said. I could feel the pain and rage coming off him like the heat from a campfire.

LAST WRITES

I saw Daddy's forearms tense. Cars pulled into the parking lot and left the parking lot as the four of them stood there. I could smell the grease from the ancient griddle in back of the old restaurant. I didn't know what kind of gun Red was carrying, but I knew what guns could do.

"Not here, Red. Please," Daddy said. It didn't sound like he was begging. It sounded like he was getting ready to fight, but knew it was pointless.

"Fuck your son, Ant. Fuck your wife. And fuck you. Two years? Two fucking years? You think I'm stupid? Come on now. You coming with us," Red said. His fleshy face was trembling like he was straining to lift some enormous weight. He moved in front of my daddy, his back to me.

I slid over the gearshift into the driver's seat. I didn't know I was going to do it until I was lifting my right leg over the 8-Ball. Red was glaring at Daddy. The other two men with him were scanning the parking lot. Daddy was looking over Red's shoulder. He was looking at me.

"You gonna regret that," Daddy said.

I eased the parking brake down.

"I ain't gonna tell you again, Ant," Red said. The words had to struggle to get out of his clenched lips.

I pushed the clutch in with my left foot and put the car in first.

"No, I don't think you is," Daddy said.

I hit the gas as hard as I could with my right foot. Daddy had been teaching me how to drive since before I could walk. I could remember him sitting me in his lap and racing down the highway on a lazy Sunday after we had dropped Mama off at church. He'd let me drive down the lane. I'd steer while he shifted gears and worked the gas. And the Duster had a clutch that was as smooth as a high-class hooker's ass.

Daddy waited until the last minute to jump out of the way. The milkshakes went flying as I hit Red and his boys.

I never let up on the gas. Not one bit. The car bounced and jumped as I ran over their bodies. I heard that hollow dull sound you hear when you hit a raccoon or a possum and it rolls against the undercarriage and the drive shaft.

I didn't hit the brakes until I felt the rear wheels roll over the last man in the their posse. I jerked the car hard to the left and the Duster came to a stop in front of the Tastee-Freeze counter. There were three cars parked to my right. To the left, the lot was empty except for the prone bodies of Red and his crew. Daddy had sprawled across the asphalt. He jumped to his feet and ran around the car towards Red and his boys.

My father checked the first two men. Their bodies didn't look right, their pelvises twisted into impossible angles. Their chests did not rise or fall.

Red coughed. I saw bright red spittle on his pale lips. His right arm had tire tracks across the bicep. My father dropped to his knees next him. The people in the parked cars who had been enjoying their frozen concoctions and flat burgers approached the scene cautiously. They took baby steps. They didn't seem anxious to see what was on the other side of the Duster.

They didn't hear what he said to that broken man.

"I told you not in front of my boy," Daddy said.

They didn't see my father put his hand over Red's nose and mouth.

"Somebody call the Sheriff!" he yelled. One the folks who had been creeping to the scene stopped and ran into the Tastee-Freeze. I watched Red's feet twitch—once, then twice, then no more.

Daddy stood up and came over to the car. He opened the door. "Come on, Bug. Get out. The police gonna be here soon. Don't want to give them no reason to put a bullet in your head cuz you behind the wheel of a six-thousand-pound killing machine," he said.

I wanted to hug him. I wanted to tell him I had done it for him. But I just turned my head and vomited all over the side of the car.

"It's alright boy. It's alright not to have the stomach for my kind of life," he said as he rubbed the back of my neck.

The sheriff didn't arrest me. Not right then. They came back a couple of weeks later and I ended up doing six months in juvie. I think the sheriff thought I had done him a favor. That was the only time I've ever seen the inside of a cell. But that afternoon, my daddy had told me what to say, and once I said it they let me go home. But we had to catch a ride. They impounded the Duster. They did let us get our groceries out of it though. We got back to the trailer and Daddy told Mama the story we had sold to the cops.

"The boy got in the driver's seat and was messing around with the pedals. It was my fault really. I was the one left it running. He accidentally hit the clutch and the car took off," he had said.

My mother had lit up a smoke and crossed her toned legs.

"Get the fuck out my house, Anthony," she said before exhaling a plume of blue-gray smoke.

"You a hard woman, Jean. It ain't worth getting to parts of you that's soft cause you so damn hard," he said. He dropped down to one knee. He put his big strong hands on my shoulders.

"Remember what I told you, Bug. I love you. You the best thing that ever happened to me," he said.

My mother snorted when he had said the last part.

"I love you too, Daddy," I said. My voice sounded paper-thin.

"I'll see you soon, boy," he said. He kissed me on the cheek. He smelled like smoke and beer and aftershave. "Be easy on him, Jean. Don't take out what you feel for me on him."

My mother blew smoke his way. Daddy shook his head and headed for the door. I'd like to say he looked back one last time, but he wasn't built like that.

Daddy had snitched on Blue. I think I knew it that day in the parking lot, but had it confirmed years later. He did his two years, but he didn't come back when he got out of Mecklenburg. He called once and said he was going west. We never heard from him again. When my mother was real good and drunk—which was more often than not— she would point at me with the glowing tip of her cigarette and tell me I was a fool.

"You think you saved him that day? You just postponed the inevitable," she would say. She would stretch out the syllables in the word "inevitable" because she knew it irritated me.

My dad's momma had gotten the Duster out of the impound and parked it at her house until I turned sixteen and got my license. I had inherited my father's talent for turning wrenches as well as his car. I had it up and running a week after I was legal. Eventually I got my own garage and stored it there.

"You would never consider selling it?" the customer asked.

"No," I said.

He looked at it longingly again. "Too bad. It's cherry," he said.

I crossed my arms. "Let's talk about the car you *have* purchased. 2009 Cadillac DTS. Modified fuel injector with turbo overdrive. Run-flat tires. Armor plating on all four doors and a back plate behind the grill. Bulletproof glass.

Ghost plates and fake serial number. When we dump it, they will never be able to trace it," I said.

The customer was still looking at the Duster. "I hope you live up to your reputation," he said.

I shook my head. "I don't have a reputation because I don't get caught. I have credentials. I have satisfied customers. Barroom brawlers have reputations," I said.

"Was your old man a wheelman too?" the customer asked.

"I'll see you Friday," I said. I turned and started to walk back to the truck.

"What about ten grand?" he asked.

I didn't even pause my stride.

"It's not for sale," I said. I guess I could have told him how I sit in that car sometimes without turning over the engine. I grip the steering wheel and I take deep long breaths. I could have told him how I sit there and think of the last time I saw my daddy. I think of the last time we rode in that car together.

The engine had sounded like a pride of lions. The seats had been as soft as a baby's laughter. We had been sitting on a rocket waiting for it to explode. In my daydreams, he turns to me and asks if I'm afraid.

I always say, "Not if you're not."

And he says, "That's my boy."

He's always a better person in the daydream than he could have ever been in real life.

But then again, aren't we all?

AUTHOR BIOS

PATRICK COOPER is a writer from Jersey whose crime fiction has appeared in *Thuglit, Spinetingler, Shotgun Honey, Dark Corners, Out of the Gutter,* and more. He'll have a ginger ale, thanks.

S.A. COSBY is a writer from southeastern Virginia. His work has been published in several anthologies and magazines including *Thuglit.* His fantasy novel *The Brotherhood of the Blade* was published in 2014 by HCS Publishing. He recently completed his first crime novel *My Darkest Prayer.* He lives in Gloucester VA with his pug Pugsley and a cantankerous squirrel named Solomon.

AARON FOX-LERNER was born in Los Angeles and currently lives in Beijing. His fiction has appeared in *Thuglit, The Puritan, Crime Factory,* Akashic Books online, *Shotgun Honey,* and other publications.

NICK KOLAKOWSKI lives and writes in New York City. His crime fiction has appeared in *Shotgun Honey, Thuglit, Crime Syndicate Magazine,* and *Out of the Gutter.* His novella *A Brutal Bunch of Heartbroken Saps* is due later this year from One Eye Press. If this whole writing thing doesn't work out, he may consider stealing boats for a living.

BLAIR KROEBER is a fiction and screenwriter residing in Los Angeles, the city of sunshine and shadow.

NICK MANZOLILLO's short fiction has previously appeared in the online publications *Nebula Rift* and *Iberian* magazine. He recently received his B.A in English from the University of Rhode Island. He is currently earning a master's degree in creative and professional writing from

Western Connecticut State University. He lives in Manhattan, NYC.

MIKE MCCRARY is the author of *Remo Went Rogue* and *Getting Ugly*. He's been a waiter, a securities trader, dishwasher, investment manager and an unpaid Hollywood intern. He's quit corporate America, come back, been fired, been promoted, been fired again. Currently he writes stories about questionable people who make questionable decisions. Keep up with Mike at mikemccrary.com.

ANDREW PAUL's work has been featured in, or coming out with *Virginia Quarterly Review*, *Oxford American*, *The Bitter Southerner*, *The Believer*, *Tablet*, and *VICE*. Another short story is forthcoming in *Mississippi Noir* (Akashic Books, August 2016), edited by Tom Franklin.

Stephen King was **DALE PHILLIPS'** college writing teacher. Since then, Dale has published the Zack Taylor mystery series, a supernatural thriller novel, over sixty short stories, story collections, poetry, and a non-fiction career book on interviewing. His stories have been published in a number of anthologies with other writers. He's a speaker with the Sisters in Crime, and is also in the New England Horror Writers.

JAMES QUEALLY is a crime reporter for the Los Angeles Times, but he writes fiction because facts and attribution aren't any goddamn fun sometimes. His short fiction has appeared in *All Due Respect*, *Shotgun Honey*, *Literary Orphans*, *Crime Syndicate Magazine*, *Out Of The Gutter Online* and *Dark Corners*. He's from Coney Island, a.k.a. the part of Brooklyn the hipsters haven't fucked up yet.

WILLIAM SOLDAN lives in the Rustbelt city of Youngstown, Ohio, with his wife and son and received his BA in English from Youngstown State University. He is currently a student in the Northeast Ohio MFA program and teaches English Composition at YSU. His work has appeared or is forthcoming in a number of publications such as *The Fictioneer, Floyd County Moonshine, New World Writing, The Vignette Review, Thuglit, Flash Fiction Magazine, Elm Leaves Journal* and others. You can follow him on Twitter @RustWriter1 or find him on Facebook (as Bill Soldan).

KYLE SUMMERALL is a recent graduate of the Mississippi University for Women and Men. His fiction has appeared twice in *The Dilletanti*, where both pieces earned either an honorable mention, and in the most recent issue, won third place overall. He's also been published in both the September and January Edition of *Writing Raw Magazine* 2015 and 2016. He hopes to join the long line of great southern writers like Faulkner, Brown, Hannah, and Gay. The south and its traditions mean a lot to Kyle and this story.

TODD ROBINSON (Editor) is the creator and Chief Editor of *Thuglit*. His writing has appeared in *Blood & Tacos, Plots With Guns, Needle Magazine, Shotgun Honey, Strange, Weird, and Wonderful, Out of the Gutter, Pulp Pusher, Grift, Demolition Magazine, CrimeFactory, All Due Respect*, and several anthologies. He has been nominated three times for the Derringer Award, selected for *Best American Mystery Stories* and *Writers Digest*'s Year's Best Writing 2003, lost the Anthony Award both in 2013 AND 2014, and won the inaugural Bullet Award in June 2011. The first collection of his short stories, *Dirty Words* and his debut novel *The Hard Bounce* are now available and his upcoming novel, *Rough Trade* will be released by Polis Books in 2016.

ALLISON GLASGOW (Editor) will cut your pretty *face.*

JULIE MCCARRON (Editor) is a celebrity ghostwriter with three New York Times bestsellers to her credit. Her books have appeared on every major entertainment and television talk show; they have been featured in *Publishers Weekly* and excerpted in numerous magazines including

People. Prior to collaborating on celebrity bios, Julie was a book editor for many years. Julie started her career writing press releases and worked in the motion picture publicity department of Paramount Pictures and for Chasen & Company in Los Angeles. She also worked at General Publishing Group in Santa Monica and for the Dijkstra Literary Agency in Del Mar before turning to editing/writing full-time. She lives in Southern California.

43135742R00114